A Place Called Jeopardy

Matt Turner figured even a lawman had the right to take things easier as he got older. But then Duke Coulter arrived in town, a man with ambition and no scruples, with a handful of hired guns to make sure nobody got in his way. Suddenly Jeopardy wasn't Matt's town any more; people were dying and there didn't seem to be a thing he could do about it.

Pretty soon Matt was losing his friends, and a man called Logan was wearing the sheriff's badge. Matt found himself with a price on his head, running for his life. If he was going to bring justice back to Jeopardy, he would have to fight on the other side of the law.

A Place Called Jeopardy

Eugene Clifton

A Black Horse Western

ROBERT HALE · LONDON

ISBN 978-0-7090-8487-7

Robert Hale Limited
Clerkenwell House
Clerkenwell Green
London EC1R 0HT

www.halebooks.com

To Val,
who shared so many of
those hours in the saddle

Typeset by
Derek Doyle & Associates, Shaw Heath
Printed and bound in Great Britain by
Antony Rowe Limited, Wiltshire

CHAPTER ONE

Sheriff Matt Turner plunged into the dimly lit saloon. Unable to see much, his ears told him that at least a dozen men were fighting, while a rowdy crowd of bystanders shouted encouragement and stomped their feet on the floor. Clouds of dust rose to mingle with the haze of tobacco smoke.

There was a flickering glow from a lamp at the top of the stairs; Duke Coulter had given orders that lights were to be doused when a fight broke out, common sense since the Royal Flush down the street had burnt to the ground during a similar ruckus less than a year ago. Trouble was it meant Matt could make out nothing but a shadowy mass of heaving bodies in the centre of the room.

Behind the sheriff, Two Shots gave a throaty chuckle. 'You want this?'

With a sigh Matt nodded and reached for the shotgun the old man held. Before he could take it something heavy was flung across the high counter, the squeal of pain as it hit the back wall telling him the projectile was human. By a stroke of bad luck the man hit the mirror and, with a crack as loud as a gunshot, the glass shattered into a thousand pieces.

There was a brief pause, but Matt made the most of it. 'That's enough!' His roar sent men flinching back, the level of noise dropping so he could hear the tinkling sound as the last shards of glass hit the floor. Silence fell, but for a breathy groan as a man rolled away from his opponent's hold, followed by stealthy scurrying footsteps. A few prudent souls were abandoning the fight to hide among the spectators.

'You, behind the bar, give us some light. Now!' Matt bellowed, as the shadowy figure hesitated.

There was the scrape of a match and a flicker of flame. Seconds later the light steadied and Matt could see the remaining combatants. Jed Whittaker was rising to his feet, hands held out placatingly. The two men he'd been grappling with a moment before stayed on the floor. Both wore identical bib-fronted overalls which, along with a discarded cap crushed under Jed's foot, identified them as railroad engineers. It was the younger man who had groaned; he was gingerly feeling his ribs, his face white.

On the edges of the light a couple more men slipped furtively into the crowd of onlookers. Matt let them go. He had more than enough to deal with. In the centre of the room two men were leaning into a wrestling hold, foot to foot and breast to breast. They were oblivious of the sheriff's presence, silently intent on killing each other.

It should have been an uneven match; Monty Caine was five foot nine and slightly built, while his opponent was a giant, maybe six five, and weighing in twice as heavy as the cowboy from the Circle T, but Monty had his forearm locked across the big man's throat and his face was turning purple. Even so, Matt wouldn't have given long odds on the cowboy's eventual victory; his body was bending backwards slowly but inexorably. Under the pressure of the giant's crushing weight his spine surely curving way beyond where it was meant to go.

'You want me to split 'em up?' Two Shots asked, lifting the shotgun.

'No, I'll . . .' Matt never got to finish the sentence. He didn't see exactly how Monty freed himself, but he thrust away from the big man, a whoop of relief escaping from between bruised lips. He came pounding back in before the giant even realized he'd gone, his left fist swinging up to make contact with the man's jaw. As the huge head snapped back, the cowboy followed up with a right fist travelling so fast it was a blur, sinking the blow deep below his adversary's breastbone. With a strange sound like the creak of over-worked bellows, the giant fell to the floor and lay still.

'Monty . . .' Matt was moving, cautiously edging round, making himself some space. If the cowboy had been drinking he wouldn't come quietly. The younger man, eyes afire, stared back at him, the corners of his mouth lifted in a savage grin. There was no sign of recognition on his battered face.

'Monty, that's enough, kid.' Matt's words fell on deaf ears, and he sent a quick glance at Jed Whittaker, hoping for some help. The two men were long-time partners, working together at Will Trent's place for the last three years. Jed gave a helpless shrug; with a shot or two of whiskey inside him Monty Caine was a formidable fighter, and as likely to try to kill a friend as an enemy.

Matt sighed, clenching his fists and loosening his shoulder muscles. He was getting too old for this. Maybe the folks who said it was time Jeopardy had a new lawman were right.

He met the young cowpoke's first rush head on, ducking at the last second to get under Monty's left, and landing a stinging blow which took the power out of the younger man's right. They sparred briefly, trading knock for knock, Monty backing away, the crowd giving ground a step at a time and closing up behind them, jeering and shouting encouragement as the mood took them.

Four men sat playing poker as if no disturbance was taking place, their table placed close to the stairs, handily under the one lamp always kept alight. Jerking back from Matt's cautious left jab, Monty avoided the blow but crashed into Doc Gardino's chair, breaking the back off and splintering one leg. The cowboy almost lost his balance as he jumped away from the wreckage, but the doctor went down, his cards still clutched in his hand.

Pressing hard, making the most of his minute advantage, Matt followed Monty back to the centre of the room. As the cowboy swung to one side trying to get past his guard Matt found himself facing the poker players again. Despite his precarious position he couldn't hold back a grin as he saw Doc Gardino pick up the broken chair, prop what was left of the back under the broken leg then sit down to go on with the game.

As he dodged a haymaker that grazed his ear, Matt knew he was close to finished; his heart was pounding way too fast for comfort, and his breathing was beginning to rasp painfully in his chest. He couldn't afford to let the fight go on, or he'd be stretching his length on the floor beside the huge railroad man. Gathering himself for one conclusive effort he leapt back and aside, reducing the impact of Monty's fresh attack, though the cowboy's deadly right still made thudding contact with his ribcage.

The sheriff had only a split second before Monty moved in to finish him. He slipped a hand into the pocket of his vest. Swaying as if the cowboy's last blow had winded him, he twisted suddenly with the speed and grace of a well-trained cowpony. Lifting his right hand he brought it down hard alongside Monty's ear. The cowboy went over without even a whimper. Gasping for breath, the sheriff bent forward, resting his hands briefly on his knees until the room steadied.

Two Shots sidled up alongside him. 'He almost had you that time,' the old man whispered.

More lamps were lit, and Matt straightened up. It was a lawman's duty not only to quell a breach of the peace, but to seek out its cause. He scanned the crowd, looking for a reliable witness, trying to sort out where the trouble had started. The man whose head had smashed the mirror to splinters was climbing groggily to his feet. Duke Coulter was going to want payment for the damage, but he'd be looking elsewhere. The battered face that appeared over the bar belonged to Mendez, one of Coulter's own men.

Matt's gaze moved on and came to rest on an open-faced youngster with a shock of fair hair. The sheriff smiled as he walked across the room towards the boy. Nobody knew exactly how old Billy was, around seventeen perhaps; a year working for Kurt Jensen at the black-smith's forge had filled him out, broadening chest and shoulders so he looked older.

'You see what happened, Billy?' Matt asked.

The youngster nodded.

'So who started it? I guess it was Monty?'

Billy shook his head.

'You sure, son? It's always Monty. Don't tell me it was Jed?'

Another shake, more vehement this time, his gaze sliding past the sheriff.

'The railroad men?'

Billy bit his lip then lifted his index finger.

'Just one of them,' Matt ventured.

This brought a vigorous nod, and Billy pointed to the big man who still lay unconscious on the floor.

Matt raised his eyebrows. 'Him. He started the fight?'

Billy nodded again, his mouth opening at last. 'Eh,' he said firmly.

'OK.' Matt turned back to where Two Shots had the shotgun pointing vaguely in the direction of the two railroad engineers. 'Pick up your buddy,' he said. 'You can all cool your heels for a few hours. And unless you boys have got a lot of back pay in your pockets we'll wait for your boss to come and pay your dues.'

Struggling a little under the weight, the two men obediently carried their friend, now snoring softly, out of the door. Without waiting to be told, Jed Whittaker heaved the unconscious Monty on to his back and followed.

Yawning widely, Matt began to stretch as he took his first lungful of morning air, but a jolt of pain from a cracked rib stopped him. He turned away from the sunny street and walked through the two-roomed shack which he called home. It wasn't much, but being beside his office it was real handy. Out back he visited the privy then returned to kick at the door of the ramshackle lean-to propped against the back wall.

'Two Shots, get your lazy hide out of there. I need you to go down to the depot. Reckon they'll be needing those two men when the freight comes through. Tell the boss man to come see me. And on your way back you can find Billy.'

With a cup of strong coffee inside him Matt felt ready to face Duke Coulter when he came striding into the office a few minutes later. Coulter wasn't alone. Logan, the new man who had turned up a couple of weeks ago, followed a pace behind. A hatchet-faced individual with short cropped hair and a permanently shadowed jaw, Logan stared at Matt balefully, staying silent as his boss wished the sheriff a cheerful good morning.

Matt returned the saloon-owner's greeting, wondering briefly where these two had been during the fight; it wasn't like Duke to be absent when there was money to be made, and the Blue Diamond had been doing a roaring trade.

'You know why I'm here,' Coulter said, seating himself in the visitor's chair without waiting to be asked. 'That mirror wasn't cheap. I'll have to send back East for a replacement. Shipping alone could cost thirty bucks.'

'You'll need to talk to the railroad; I doubt if the three men I've got locked up back there have got thirty bucks between them.'

'Three men? I heard it was five.'

'Yeah, but Monty and Jed are only in jail while they sleep it off. It was the railroad men who started the fight.'

'That's not what I heard.' Coulter's tone was suddenly cold. 'Caine starts fights the way other men say howdy.'

'Not this time.' The two men locked gazes across the desk. 'If you don't believe me, we can wait until the judge comes round. Be another two months, seeing he's always late, and I don't reckon folks will be too happy about the town paying to keep five men in jail all that time, but if that's the way you want it . . .'

'Maybe you won't be here in two months' time.' Logan spoke for the first time, his voice pitched low.

'Now, Logan,' Duke Coulter smiled, leaning back so his chair was balanced on two legs, 'You don't want to give Sheriff Turner the wrong idea.'

'Oh, I think I got the gist of what he said,' Matt replied evenly.

'Maybe you did.' Coulter pushed suddenly forward again, the chair crashing back to the ground. 'Logan was just reminding you about the election, weren't you, Logan?'

'Sure,' Logan growled. 'What else?'

The door opened and Two Shots rolled in, holding the door open for a tall, thin character, dressed in a smart black suit.

'This here's Mr Roper,' Two Shots said. 'Seems he's in charge down at the depot now.'

'Not exactly,' Roper replied, sweeping his black hat from his head and offering the sheriff his hand. 'I'm actually on my way to the end of the line, but I heard a couple of our engineers were in trouble, so I offered to come and see what could be done. I believe you have them locked up, Sheriff.'

Matt raised an eyebrow. 'Figured you'd be missing three men, not two,' he said. 'Though could be it's just coincidence they ended up fighting on the same side. You'd best come take a look.' He rose and opened the door through to the jail. Roper followed him, Coulter and Logan tagging along uninvited.

'O'Malley!' Roper stopped short at the sight of the big man, who had recovered sufficiently from Monty's knockout punch to sit on one of the cell's two bunks.

'So, he's one of your engineers, like them,' Matt said, nodding at the other two men in the cell who sat silent on a bunk opposite the giant. He had the feeling that Roper's surprise at seeing the man was an act put on for his benefit, though he could think of no reason why that should be so.

'No, O'Malley isn't an engineer, he's more a factotum. He's travelling with me.'

'A fac-totum,' Matt repeated, savouring the sound. 'My, that sure is a mouthful. Well, Mr Roper, this here fac-totum of yours got himself caught up in what we'll call an altercation, seeing as you like long words. And during the course of that there alter-cation, he broke Mr Coulter's mirror.'

Roper turned. 'You'll be Mr Coulter,' he said. Again, Matt had the feeling the man was acting a part, that he knew perfectly well who the saloon owner was.

Duke Coulter nodded. 'I still have the original receipt for the mirror. But to tell the truth, I haven't heard any proof that it was your man who was responsible for the breakage. The two in the other cell are a couple of well-known local troublemakers, could be the whole thing was their fault.'

'I've got a reliable witness tells it different,' the sheriff said. 'If you gentlemen would like to step back into the office I figure he'll be here any time. Two Shots, you'd better see to our prisoners, they'll maybe want a drink.'

'Sure.' Two Shots grinned. 'I'll fetch some water.'

'Water?' O'Malley jumped to his feet. 'Ain't you even gonna give a man a cup of coffee?'

'The town's kinda mean when a man's in jail,' Two Shots replied. 'You want coffee it's extra.'

'Two Shots,' Matt said warningly, 'I told you before about that. One of these days you'll get your head screwed right off at the neck if you josh the prisoners that way. Give 'em coffee. And send to the hotel for some breakfast, if any of 'em can stomach it.' He glanced at Monty, who was sitting hunched up on his bunk, nursing his head in his hands. 'Reckon you won't need to bother with him yet awhile.'

When they stepped back into the outer office Billy was waiting for them. He wore a blacksmith's apron, and he was fidgeting a little as he stared out of the window, turning a horseshoe nail over and over in his hands.

'Don't fret, Billy,' Matt Turner told him, taking the youngster by the elbow, 'I'll talk to Kurt, he won't mind you being here.'

The young man shook his head and his throat tightened as he struggled to force out a sound. 'Bee,' he said.

'Oh, you're busy. OK, we'll get right to it. These gentlemen want to know how that fight got started last night.'

Billy glanced at Coulter, then Logan, his mouth firmly closed.

'Go ahead,' Matt prompted. 'Act it out; you can do it.'

With another worried glance at Coulter's hired gun, the youngster obeyed. He took a couple of steps, bowlegged like a cowboy, acted pouring a drink and swallowing a mouthful, then leant against the window, as if at the bar of the saloon. There was total silence as he acted out the arrival of the three railroad men, somehow seeming to grow by several inches as he became O'Malley, shouldering Monty aside and knocking his whiskey over.

'Maybe it was an accident,' Duke Coulter said.

Billy screwed up his face, sweat breaking out on his forehead as he made the effort to speak. 'Ng-aa.' He was emphatic, shaking his head. After thinking for a moment he took some scraps of metal out of the pocket of his apron, choosing a big nail to represent O'Malley, a smaller one for Monty. Two more became the railroad engineers, coming at the cowboy from either side.

Logan laughed suddenly, harsh and loud. 'You ain't tellin' me you call this evidence? I got a horse with more brains. How much did you pay this half-wit, Sheriff? Shame he can't do nothin' but grunt. Hell, that's a real good name for him. Any more tricks you can do, Grunt? That horse of mine—'

He broke off suddenly, his head jerking up as the cold, hard barrel of a Colt .45 was thrust against the side of his neck.

14

CHAPTER TWO

'Just what are you suggesting?' Matt Turner's voice was as chilly as the barrel of the gun boring into Logan's neck. 'You think I'd pay a witness? I'm no liar, and neither is young Billy here.'

'It was a joke,' Duke Coulter put in smoothly. 'Tell him, Logan.'

'Sure,' Logan said, his tone surly. 'If you say so, boss.'

'Wasn't talking to your boss.' Matt applied a little more pressure, making Logan's head jerk. 'Be real sad if this gun went off by accident, a man's finger gets twitchy when he's riled. Reckon you'd best apologize.'

'I was kiddin' around.' Logan sounded less sure of himself. 'Didn't mean nothin'. Sorry if you took it the wrong way, Sheriff, you too, kid.'

'His name's Billy,' Matt prompted.

'Sure,' Logan said again, his voice rising as his breathing laboured. 'Sorry, Billy. No hard feelin's, huh?'

Matt stepped away from Logan and holstered his gun. 'Fine. Well, Mr Roper, seems like it was your men who started all this, so they pay for Mr Coulter's mirror. Since they don't have the money . . .' He paused, lifting his eyebrows questioningly.

'The company will pay,' Roper said hastily. There was a thin film of sweat on his forehead and he blinked rapidly, meeting the sheriff's gaze briefly before his glance flickered down to Matt's gunbelt. 'There's really no need for any unpleasantness.'

'Fine.' Duke Coulter rose to his feet. 'Come to the Blue Diamond with me, Mr Roper. We'll settle things over a drink.'

'You'll release the men?' Roper queried, turning back to the sheriff.

'Soon as their fine's paid. Ten dollars each for disturbing the peace. If you'd rather these three have their day in court then you can pay bail and wait for the judge's next visit, but that won't be for a couple of weeks.'

Roper took out a billfold and passed over the money, withdrawing his hand quickly as if to avoid any contact with the lawman.

'I take it they'll be leaving town real soon?' Matt asked, writing out a receipt.

'Of course. My train's scheduled to leave in half an hour. I'll arrange for Dillerby and Grice to drive the locomotive instead of taking the overnight freight, and O'Malley will be travelling with me.'

'Good. Then I'll hold on to Monty for a while, just in case he's still feeling sore. Be grateful if you'd keep your men on a tighter rein from now on, Roper.'

Duke Coulter ushered the railroad man out into the street. Logan followed his boss, half turning as if to keep an eye on the sheriff. 'Reckon I won't be turnin' my back on you no more,' he ground out.

Matt nodded. 'I'll bear that in mind.' When the door had closed he grinned at Billy. 'Thanks, Billy. You know, it's a real shame nobody ever taught you to write.'

Two Shots guffawed. 'What good would that be? Can't be more'n a dozen people in Jeopardy who know how to read.'

'One would be enough,' Matt said mildly. 'How about it, Billy? Maybe we could fix for you to have some lessons, then it'd be a whole lot easier when you wanted to tell folks something.'

The youngster shrugged. He picked up the nails from the sheriff's desk and pointed at them with his other hand.

'Sure, I know you're happy working for Kurt,' Matt said, clapping Billy on the shoulder as he saw him out of the door. 'But you could still do that. If you change your mind let me know.'

'Be a damn waste of anybody's time teachin' a half-wit to read,' Two Shots commented, once they were alone.

'Maybe that's why nobody taught you,' Matt replied. 'There's nothing wrong with Billy's brain; it's only his voice that don't work. Get me some coffee, then go let those three out. Once they've gone I'll have a word with Monty, I'm getting too old to put him down most every week.'

'You hopin' he'll sign the pledge?'

Matt sighed, wincing as he straightened his back. 'I guess that's pretty unlikely, though it sure would make my life easier.'

Three days later, Matt was still feeling the effects of his battle with Monty. It was an effort not to limp as he made his way down the street to the railroad depot.

'You meeting somebody, Sheriff?' Clive Pechey, the railroad clerk, strolled across to intercept him. 'Train's on time, be here in five minutes.'

'Just keeping an eye on things.' Young Billy was seated

on Kurt Jensen's buckboard, alongside the line where the freight car would stop. 'They finally expecting that new shaft for the mill?'

'So I hear.' Pechey tipped his head in the other direction. 'Could be some more interesting cargo aboard, too.' Duke Coulter's smart two-horse rig was drawn up nearby, Logan slouching over the reins, while his boss sat behind him on the sprung leather-covered seat, leaning forward with his hands resting on a black cane.

'Turned himself out real fancy,' Pechey went on. 'Logan don't look too happy. Could be Mr Coulter's bringing in more help, he's getting to be a big man around these parts, maybe he's expecting some extra muscle.'

'Muscle I got no problem with,' Matt said, 'but the last thing Jeopardy needs is more hired guns.'

'Folks say Duke's making a move to take over Winner's Seed and Grain. What with the stockyard and the mill, reckon he'll own half of Jeopardy before he's through.' The clerk gave Matt a sidelong glance. 'I heard he's putting Logan forward for the election next month.'

'I heard that too,' Matt said mildly.

'Well, I can't see him getting many votes, Sheriff,' Pechey said, turning to get back to his work. 'As long as you're in office the town's in good hands.'

Matt shifted his stance, silently cursing Monty for his aches and pains, though if he was honest they weren't all due to the cowboy's fists. A man couldn't go on taking the same kind of punishment with nearly forty-five summers behind him. The people of Jeopardy had supported him for fifteen years, but Coulter wasn't the only one talking about needing new blood when it came to the enforcement of law in the town. The way he'd felt crawling out of bed that morning he'd begun to wonder if they were right.

18

Only five people got off the train, and none of them looked like a gunslinger. Duke Coulter climbed down from his rig to meet two women. The older one was a peroxide blonde dressed in emerald satin. Her plentiful hair was crowned with a matching green bonnet. The brightness of the day wasn't kind to her; once she might have been a beauty, but the passage of years had left their mark on her face and her figure. She was left with the kind of blowsy good looks that are best seen only by lamplight.

Matt shook his head in disbelief; he'd known Duke had plans for the Blue Diamond, but he'd never thought Sally Schott would leave her own place in Serena. One thing was sure, Jeopardy would be a whole lot rowdier from now on. Sally played piano pretty well and she wasn't a bad singer, but what she did best was stir things up, especially in a place where men outnumbered women two to one. The way Matt heard it, she was only happy when half Serena's townsfolk were at each other's throats.

Matt's gaze wandered to the second new arrival, and all thoughts of Sally Schott were instantly forgotten. The girl was simply dressed, her clothes more suited to a high-class schoolmarm than a saloon girl, but she had large dark eyes that roved boldly across the few male residents of Jeopardy who were out and about that morning. Her figure was perfect, curvy in all the right places, and with a waist so narrow Matt's hands would have fitted around it. She swayed seductively against Logan as he helped her into the carriage beside Sally. Once she was seated, the girl swivelled to look appraisingly at Will Trent, who was loading his wagon outside the store. The rancher saluted her with a grin, touching his hat with one finger, and was rewarded with a coquettish toss of the head. This girl was no schoolmarm.

Logan climbed to the box, sitting upright now instead of slouching. He turned the horses and urged them to a smart trot, but the girl didn't seem to be watching him. Her gaze flickered over Matt and dismissed him, but not before he'd seen the wide sultry mouth, painted red so the lips contrasted with the small white teeth.

Matt turned to see who had earned her smile. His heart sank. There was Billy, tall and well-muscled, his fair hair showing off his healthy tan; he was smiling right back at her. She gave him a little wave, obviously enjoying the effect she'd had on such a fine, well-set-up young man. Billy was tall, strong and good to look at, she wouldn't know he was still a green kid. Or that he couldn't speak a single word.

Once Duke Coulter's rig had taken the new arrivals swiftly out of his sight Billy hurried to Matt, his mouth working as he struggled to form a word.

Boo . . .' he managed at last. 'Sh . . . ee . . .' Matt had never known the youngster lose patience with his dumbness before, but now he slapped his thigh in frustration.

'Yes,' Matt said, 'you're right, kid, she sure is beautiful.' He laid a heavy hand on Billy's arm and turned him around. 'There's nothing for you there,' he said. 'You don't want to go mooning after saloon girls. Get on home; Kurt will be waiting for that shaft.'

The day cooled as it moved towards evening and the town began to reawaken, with sounds of voices and the occasional hush of wheels coming through the open doorway. Matt finished his game of solitaire and put the soiled old cards back in his desk drawer. It would soon be time to close the office and make his rounds.

The soft thud of hoofs sent him to the door. Three horses were approaching, the first of them a grey, bright in the last light from the sun. Its rider was swaying in the saddle, holding to the horn as if he'd fall without its support. In a slack hand he held the reins of two more horses, one of them pulling a roughly made travois, the other carrying a man who sat hunched forward, his hands clasped together in front of him.

As the sheriff reached him the lead rider tipped sideways and began to fall. Matt caught him, lowering him to the ground and shouting for Two Shots. The second rider was suddenly in motion, bending forward then jerking upright, slapping his heels madly at the horse's flanks and urging it into motion. Matt had to jump aside to avoid being trampled, and as he did so, he saw the man's hands were tied to the saddle horn. When he leant down it had been to grasp the trailing rein in his teeth.

'Stop him!' A figure half rose from the travois only to sink back with a groan of pain. 'Jeez, Matt, get after the bastard!'

Matt grabbed the grey horse's reins, ready to swing into the saddle but there was no need. From along the street he heard a whoop. Monty Caine and Jed Whittaker swept across from outside the blacksmith's shop, their horses fresh and ready to run. The fugitive never had a chance.

'Jay, that you?' Matt went to look down at the man lying on the travois. Marshal Jay Brand scowled back up at him.

'Who else does it look like? How's Bert?' He strained to rise so he could see the man now lying on Matt's veranda.

Two Shots appeared from somewhere, rubbing the back of his hand across his mouth as he wove an unsteady path towards them.

'Go get Doc Gardino,' Matt ordered, lifting the fallen man, 'and make it fast.'

'You reckon he'll get there?' Brand asked, as Two Shots zigzagged away.

'Two Shots works best when he's half full of whiskey,' Matt replied. 'What happened? This kid's burning up real bad.'

'His name's Bert Dobson. He took sick last night. Wasn't a damn thing I could do to help, stuck on this contraption with my leg bust. First time I've ridden with him. He's kinda young to be a marshal, but he's done real well. I don't know how he held out to get us here.'

Matt carried the youngster into his office. Monty and Jed followed him in, pushing the recaptured prisoner before them.

'Be obliged if you'd lock him up,' Matt said, lowering the young marshal into his chair and nodding towards the keys on his desk.

'My pleasure,' Monty replied, grimacing, 'sure feels good to be the right side of the bars for a change.'

'I'll take you on as deputy any time,' Matt returned, wringing out a cloth to cool the sick man's face, 'just as soon as you sign the pledge.'

With the prisoner safely in a cell, the two cowboys lifted Jay Brand off the travois and fetched him inside, sitting him on the floor beside his partner. 'Where's that damn doc?' Brand demanded.

'That damn doc is right here,' Gardino said, coming through the door. 'What is this, a travelling hospital?'

'Who's the prisoner?' Matt asked. The doctor had gone, taking Bert Dobson with him so he could have proper care. Marshal Brand was lying on a bedroll in Matt's tiny shack, his leg set and splinted, and his face pale under its deep tan.

'Harve Rawlins. I tell you, Matt, I never had such a run of bad luck. Rawlins killed a man in Kansas City back in the fall. It took six of us to run him down, but we got him in the end. He was tried and sentenced three months ago, then damn me if he didn't go and escape just two days before he was due to hang.

'Wasn't time to put a posse together. I'd only just met Bert but there wasn't no other marshals around, and the kid offered to come along and keep me company. He's earned his keep sure enough. We've been on Rawlins' trail so long I feel like I've known him all my life.'

'Doc's a good man, reckon the kid'll be ready to travel before you are.'

'I was thinking about that. Look, Matt, could you help out? With a reliable deputy you could take Rawlins back to Kansas City for me.'

'It's not a good time, Jay. Nearest thing I've got to a deputy is Two Shots. And I'm coming up for re-election in two weeks. I'll keep your man safe though, for as long as it takes.'

Brand sighed. 'Guess that'll have to do. But Rawlins is one slippery character. Sure would be mad if he got away from me again.'

Jeopardy dozed in the afternoon sun. It was stiflingly hot, and Matt was sitting in the ancient chair on the veranda outside his office. He'd tipped his hat over his eyes, loosened his belt and slipped his feet out of his boots, and he was nearly asleep. It was thirteen days since his fight with Monty. His bruises had faded and it was no longer an effort to walk upright.

Things had been quiet since the two marshals appeared with their prisoner. It didn't look like they'd be leaving anytime soon. Jay Brand still lay in Matt's cabin, cursing the heat and his busted leg at frequent intervals, while

Dobson was still at Doc Gardino's. The fever had passed its crisis but left the young marshal so weak he couldn't yet stand without help.

As far as Matt could tell, folks were ready to vote for him at the election, but he'd be glad when it was over. He'd expected trouble from Duke Coulter, or Logan, but they'd kept out of his way, and so far Sally Schott was behaving herself too. She seemed content to play piano and sing at the Blue Diamond, not stirring up any unrest among the men who crowded around seeking her favours.

The girl who'd arrived with her worked in the bar most nights, dealing faro and serving drinks, and now and then she'd join Sally at the piano, adding her dusky voice to Sally's richer tones, though she rarely spoke beyond what was necessary to do her job. It had been some time before Matt even learned her name; if Mirabelle was a whore she was a very discreet one.

Peering out from under his hat brim, Matt saw Billy go slipping by in the shadows on the other side of the road, as if trying not to be seen. He drew in a breath to call out to the youngster, then let it go in a sigh. Billy hadn't got over his first sight of Mirabelle; he was crazy about her. Every afternoon while Kurt was taking a siesta and he had no work to do, Billy would prowl around the back of the Blue Diamond, hoping the girl might appear on the little shaded balcony outside her room.

So far Mirabelle had treated the kid with a kind of amused indifference, but one day her patience would run out, and then Billy would get hurt. Matt sighed again, sinking deeper into his chair and drifting closer to sleep. There was nothing he could do. Billy had to learn his lessons the hard way, just like everybody else.

Waking suddenly half an hour later Matt found a

sudden cramp seizing his calves. Swearing, he leant forward to knead at the rock hard muscles with his fingers. The pain was subsiding as a shout made him look up. Kurt Jensen was racing across the street towards him. 'Sheriff, you gotta come! It's Billy!' He pointed towards the Blue Diamond. 'The kid's gonna get himself hurt!'

Matt was instantly on his feet, grabbing a boot then discarding it, pausing only to tighten his gunbelt. He ran barefoot into the street alongside Jensen. They both came to an abrupt halt, squinting up at the roof of the saloon. There, silhouetted against the bright blue sky, was a man, crouched on top of the false frontage of the Blue Diamond, nearly thirty feet above the street.

CHAPTER THREE

The man on the roof of the saloon was tall and thin. He wore no hat and, as he craned to see who was down in the street, his face was suddenly out of the shadows, dark-skinned and with features sharp as a hatchet.

'That's Logan!' Matt turned to Jensen. 'I thought you said it was Billy—'

'Hey, Sheriff!' Logan had seen them and was attempting to clamber over the fancy scrollwork on top of the roof, his voice shrill with fear. 'He's tryin' to kill me! He's gone damnfool crazy. You gotta stop him!'

Matt didn't reply, watching as the terrified man crept further along his perilous perch, crouching in front of the thin wooden façade with its peeling paint. Logan's shirt hung open. Fresh blood was splashed across his chest and clothes, though the way he was moving it didn't look as if he was badly hurt. His feet, like Matt's, were bare. He wasn't wearing a gunbelt either, which was strange; Logan was the kind of man who would keep his gun within reach, even when he was asleep. As he grabbed at the top of the name board a scrap of rotten wood came away in his grasp, leaving the words *Blue Diamond* a few letters short.

A scrabbling sound came from the other end of the

saloon roof, and the cause of Logan's terror emerged, scrambling up the shingles and across the ridge.

Billy didn't seem to notice the audience in the street below, swelling now as more townsfolk were roused out of their afternoon siesta. He was intent only on reaching Logan. Spotting his objective he clambered over the fancy scrollwork, a wordless roar of triumph coming from his throat.

Billy stood on the narrow ledge, only the width of the building separating him from Logan, who had nowhere else to run, his only means of escape a drop to the street far below. The height didn't seem to worry the young blacksmith, and, with his back to the street, Billy edged his way towards his quarry.

It wasn't only the name board that was rotten: Billy's foot struck a bad patch. Only luck and his own quick reflexes saved the boy from falling. Grabbing a sound bit of timber he clung on left-handed, swinging so his back was to the roof. He hung there, facing the crowd of onlookers, his feet searching for something that would bear his weight.

Matt bit down hard on his lip, and beside him he heard Kurt Jensen gasp. Billy's faded blue shirt and jeans were blotched with dark wet stains. In his right hand the youngster held a knife; it too was dulled, and dark red, with no reflection shining off the blade.

'Billy!' As the boy regained his footing, Matt ran across to the hitching rail, scanning the narrow porch that covered the doorway. 'Whatever's happened, I'll deal with it, I swear.' He had to find some way of putting himself between the boy and the man he was pursuing. There was a small window above the entrance that might give him a foothold.

'Please, Billy. Stay where you are, and I'll come up to you.'

For a split second the youngster looked down and met the sheriff's eyes; his own were full of a desperate anguish. Very slowly he shook his head. He stuck the bloodstained knife into his belt and started into motion again, creeping inch by inch towards Logan. Cursing, Matt unbuckled his gunbelt and tossed it back to Kurt Jensen. He swung up on to the hitching rail and from there he leapt to grasp at the roof of the porch, pulling himself up with a strength born of desperation.

Voices called encouragement, but there were plenty who jeered when he almost lost his grip. One raised a laugh, calling out, 'You ever think of joinin' the circus, Matt?'

'He's too old,' another voice put in. It sounded like Mendez. Matt gritted his teeth and reached for the windowsill.

'They'd take the kid, he's a side-show all on his own.' This brought another gust of laughter from the men clustered around Duke Coulter.

'Wait, Billy,' Matt called breathlessly, perched precariously only feet below the boy, who was still moving, and almost past him. Billy was only seconds away from the cowering Logan, and the knife was back in his hand.

'Stop him!' Logan's voice was shrill. 'You gotta help me! Duke!'

'Just wait on, Billy, please,' Matt said. 'I'm coming, boy. Don't—'

A shot rang out – the deep bark of a rifle. There was a pause, a long drawn-out breath of silence, then Billy fell, slamming against the sloping sun-bleached timber only a foot from Matt. He caught a glimpse of wide blue eyes and

28

a mouth open in a silent scream, then the body went sliding down and away, to land with a sickening thud in the street below.

Matt eased himself back to safety on the porch and stared over the edge. Duke Coulter was lowering the rifle, and he made no protest when Two Shots came up behind him and took the weapon from his hand.

Jumping down to the ground, Matt landed heavily, but he didn't notice the pain jarring through him. He stared at Billy's body, face down in the dirt. Coulter's bullet had left a messy exit wound in his back; if the boy wasn't already dead then he soon would be. Matt bent down and gently turned the body over. Feeling for a pulse and not finding one, he closed the staring eyes. The stains on Billy's shirt front almost hid the hole made by the rifle bullet, but there were no other wounds on him; wherever all that blood had come from, it wasn't his.

By the time Matt straightened up, Mendez and another of Coulter's men had helped Logan to the ground. The man came to stand beside his boss.

'I'd call that cold-blooded murder,' Matt said bleakly, looking Coulter in the eyes.

'Before you go making any accusations there's something you gotta hear, Sheriff,' Logan said, regaining his confidence now Billy was out of the way.

'You hurt?' Matt asked, taking a closer look at the red blotches on the man's clothes.

'No. The blood ain't mine, it's Mirabelle's. I was tryin' to save her.'

'Save her?'

'From Grunt here.' Logan poked at Billy's body with the toe of his boot. 'The kid went crazy, slashed her with a knife. He must've heard me comin' because when I got there he

29

was out on the balcony, lookin' like he was gonna jump. I picked her up in my arms, figurin' I'd get her to the doctor, but I was too late, she was dead. Then I guess Grunt realized I wasn't carryin' my gun. He still had the knife in his hand, an' he came back. It was like facin' a goddamn crazy man. I didn't have a hope of gettin' the knife off him. Figured I was gonna get myself killed, so I dodged around the room some then climbed up on the roof.'

'You're sure the girl's dead?' Matt asked.

'Sure I'm sure. But you go ahead an' take a look if you don't believe me.' Logan was recovering his normal truculence, though he dropped back with a scowl when Coulter moved alongside him.

'I'm sorry, Sheriff,' the saloon owner said smoothly. 'You see now why I had to shoot. I can't have a madman killing off all my employees.'

Matt shouldered him aside. 'Kurt, Two Shots, get Billy's body off the street. And hold on to that rifle until I say different. Coulter, you and Logan had better come with me.' He headed into the saloon, followed by what looked like half the town.

When Matt reached the stairs behind the bar he stopped and turned to study the crowd, sickened by the looks on the faces staring avidly back at him; nearly every man there was hoping for a look at the murdered girl. He stabbed a finger at Mendez. 'You,' he said, 'stay where you are, and don't let anyone up here. And you' – he pointed this time at a kid who was too young to be in the saloon – 'go fetch Doctor Gardino, and don't come back or I'll tan the hide off you.'

Taking two steps up Matt stopped. The kid had gone, but most of the men showed no sign of leaving. He turned, his eyes hard.

'Saloon's closed. Plenty of other places in town you can get a drink. Unless any of you folks were upstairs five minutes ago then you got no business here right now. Clear out, or so help me I'll lock up the whole lot of you even if you're twenty to a cell.'

Sally Schott stood in the doorway of a room at the end of the corridor. She seemed hardly to notice the three men, her eyes fixed on some unseeable distance, but she stepped out of Matt's way without comment.

Mirabelle wouldn't be tempting any more men with her sultry smile. She lay across a rumpled bed in a pool of blood, clad in nothing but a cotton robe. The attack had been frenzied, Matt counted six knife wounds to her neck and chest. It was hard to think while faced with her ruined beauty, but he had a job to do. He frowned, noticing that most of the wounds were to the right side. 'Let me see your hands,' he demanded, as Logan came to stand beside him.

'This is a waste of time, Sheriff,' Duke Coulter said. 'That young imbecile went crazy and killed the girl. You heard what Logan said; he tried to stop him. He was lucky he didn't end up dead, too.'

'Your hands,' Matt repeated evenly. With a shrug Logan held out his hands. Both of them were bloody, though the left palm was almost clean. 'Where's your gun?'

'In my room, back there.' Logan jerked his head. 'I was takin' a rest when I heard Mirabelle talkin' loud to somebody. She sounded kinda upset, so seein' the door wasn't shut I came along an' looked in. I saw her lyin' right there on the bed, an' I figured to see if there was anythin' I could do. Like I said, it was too late.'

'Seems a man like you might stop to pick up his gun if he thought there was trouble,' Matt said. 'Which side do you wear your holster?'

Logan slapped his left hand to his thigh. 'Here.'

Matt looked again at the terrible wounds on the girl's body. He glanced at the doorway and saw Sally Schott still standing there. 'Find something to cover her,' he said. 'Soon as the doctor's had a look see you can clean her up if you want.'

The woman nodded, her face still showing no emotion.

'What do you need the doctor for?' Coulter asked. 'She's dead.'

'Just want to know if he sees what I see,' Matt replied.

'Are you saying we can't bury her?'

'Won't take more'n a few minutes for Doc Gardino to take a look at her.'

'What the hell for?' Logan asked belligerently.

'Reckon that's my business,' Matt said, meeting Logan's eyes with a stony stare. 'I'm still sheriff, in case you'd forgot. I guess I don't need to warn you not to leave town.'

'Logan's got no reason to leave Jeopardy,' Coulter cut in.

'That's right, I ain't goin' noplace,' Logan growled. 'But I didn't do nothin', Sheriff, except nearly get myself killed tryin' to take a knife away from that crazy kid.'

'Funny thing,' Matt said 'I never knew Billy to carry a blade.'

The saloon was empty, though there were still men hanging around outside. Back in the street there was only a dark patch drying rapidly in the sun to show where Billy had lain. Two Shots came weaving his way up the street. He handed Matt his gunbelt. 'Kurt thought you'd want this.'

'Thanks.' Matt buckled the belt and drew his Colt, suddenly sickened by the whole messy business. He fired three swift shots in the air. 'You people get on home. There's nothing to see, but if you got an appetite for blood then I'll take on any one of you, right here, right now, and give you a taste of it.'

There was muttering from a couple of Coulter's men, and a burly miner spat noisily on the ground as he turned away, but within a minute Matt and Two Shots had the street to themselves.

'Kurt took Billy to the undertaker,' Two Shots said. 'He'll see he gets buried decent, even if he did end up a murderer.'

'Who says he murdered anybody?' Matt replied, his anger still close to the surface. 'Did you ever see the kid turn violent before? And where's the knife?'

'Knife?' Two Shots looked blank.

'As I recall, it lay right there beside Billy's hand. I thought maybe you'd picked it up.'

'You didn't say nothin' about a knife,' Two Shots said sulkily, 'Can't expect me to think of everythin'. You sure it was down here?' he added hopefully. 'Maybe he dropped it on the roof'

'It was here.'

'Kurt could've picked it up.'

'Or maybe one of Coulter's men has it, which means our most important piece of evidence just went missing,' Matt said. He sighed. It irked him to know Coulter was right, he was getting too old for this job.

'My fault, not yours,' he admitted. 'Anyway, there's no hope of proving Logan was the one who killed the girl, not while Duke Coulter owns half the town.'

'You figure Logan killed her?' Two Shots asked.

'We'll go and talk to Kurt, just in case. And I want to ask him what he saw. Something made him come and fetch me.'

'Maybe we ought to take a look in the office first,' Two Shots said suddenly.

Matt turned to follow the old man's gaze, and a moment later he was sprinting across the street, oblivious of the stones that cut his bare feet as he ran. His chair lay on its side in the doorway. Inside, the door to the cells stood wide open. And so did the door to Harve Rawlins's empty cell.

'I'm real sorry, Jay.' Matt hurried around the cabin, gathering up his bedroll and a fresh box of ammunition. 'I know how hard you worked to get that man back, I'll try not to let what you and Dobson did go to waste. Two Shots will be staying in town, he'll take care of you while I'm gone.'

Brand groaned. 'Sure wish I was fit to come along. And don't go blaming yourself, it wasn't no fault of yours; a man can't be in two places at once.'

'No, but he could have the dad-blamed sense to lock a door behind him! I already messed up once today. Maybe Coulter's right, I'm getting old.' He slung a bag containing coffee, biscuits and hard tack over his shoulder. 'One thing, we know what horse he stole, and it's not fast. Given luck I'll catch up with him.'

'Good hunting,' Brand called, as Matt ran out of the door. Two Shots had his horse saddled and waiting, and within a minute the sheriff was on his way, hightailing it out of town. A couple of people had seen Rawlins. They both swore he'd ridden out of Jeopardy alone, but Matt didn't see how that could be. He'd made a stupid mistake leaving the office door open and the keys to the cells inside, but there was no way Rawlins could have reached them without another man's help.

34

There was no time to look for that man now though, it was more important to put Rawlins back behind bars. And no matter what Jay Brand said, Matt knew he was to blame for the man's escape, just as he was to blame for letting the knife that killed Mirabelle disappear. Not to mention he hadn't managed to save young Billy's life.

His horse was fresh and ready to run, and Matt made good speed. He'd met a farmer driving into town for supplies, and learnt that Rawlins was heading west, riding as if the devil himself was on his heels. Likely he wouldn't stop running until he reached the mountains.

Matt was on the Circle T, Will Trent's spread, when he saw the three horsemen on the horizon. For a heart-stopping moment he wondered if Rawlins had been joined by the friends who'd let him loose; a solitary lawman would be fair game to a trio of outlaws. As he drew nearer Matt recognized one of the horses and knew he was safe for the moment; this was Will, heading out to bring his cattle to fresh pasture. The two men riding alongside him were Monty and Jed.

'Evening, Sheriff,' Trent greeted him. 'You coming to call?'

'Wish I was, Will,' Matt replied. 'I'm after that prisoner from Kansas City.' Briefly he related the events at the saloon. 'While we were looking the other way some damn coyote slipped into the jail and let Rawlins out.'

'Well, if that don't beat all.' Monty tipped back his hat. 'And after all the trouble me and Jed took catching him for you the first time.'

'Call it the third time,' Matt countered. 'That man seems to slip past the law like a goddamn eel. Well, I'd best keep moving.'

'Pretty foolhardy thing to do, riding after a murderer

all on your lonesome,' Jed commented.

'That's right.' Will Trent swung his horse around. 'Maybe I should ride along, Matt.'

'I'd be glad to have your company, Will, but what about Martha? I heard she's still no better.'

Will grimaced. 'Doc was out to see her again yesterday. I guess you're right, I can't leave her there with the boys right now.' He looked at Monty and Jed. 'These two could go with you instead; reckon I can do without them for a couple of days.'

'What do you say, Sheriff?' Monty looked at him with a challenge in his eyes. 'You said I'd make a deputy, though I ain't ready to sign the pledge yet awhiles.'

'Provided you don't bring any whiskey along,' Matt replied. 'If you're willing and your boss can spare you, that's fine by me.'

CHAPTER FOUR

'I just don't get it.' Jed Whittaker had been hunkered down, his nose only inches above the dust, now he lifted wearily to his feet. 'An hour ago we were following one horse, the trail was so plain even Monty could see it. Now we got three damn riders, going every which way like they was dancin' at a hoedown.'

'They must have come along the river-bed,' Matt said, looking down at the mess of hoof prints. 'Well, that's about the only thing I got right about this whole business: I said Rawlins had somebody helping him. They must have arranged this, that's why he suddenly headed south, to give them a chance to get out of town and join him.'

'But who would he know in Jeopardy?' Monty objected. 'You told us he's from Kansas City.'

'Maybe he didn't know anybody. Maybe somebody thought a jailbreak was a good way to stop me asking too many questions about what happened to Mirabelle and Billy. I wouldn't put it past Coulter to free a murderer just to get me off Logan's back.' He stared at the sky. 'We're losing the light; we'll camp here tonight.'

'Then what?' Jed asked.

'Then we try to figure out which set of tracks to follow.

My guess is Rawlins will still be heading west, but he'll lay a false trail for a mile or two first. If the other two riders are from Jeopardy they'll head back there. We'll split up, follow one trail each and see where they take us.'

'The way Monty follows tracks he'll likely find himself on top of the nearest anthill,' Jed said, grinning.

'That's twice you've said I can't read a trail,' Monty complained, lifting the saddle off his horse's back. 'Sure is hurtful when a friend goes running a man down.'

'Ain't runnin' you down,' Jed replied. 'Tellin' the truth is all.'

'Truth can still hurt, ain't that right, Sheriff?' Monty said.

Matt nodded, only half following what they were saying, still fretting about his failure to catch Rawlins.

'Shucks, you'll have me cryin' like a baby,' Jed shot back, as he led his horse away towards the stream.

Monty watched him go, a thoughtful expression on his face. Suddenly he smiled. 'Reckon that truth's gonna come back an' bite Jed before he's done.' He followed his friend, whistling softly.

Matt dealt with his own horse, wishing he shared the cowboy's light-heartedness. It wasn't going to be easy tracking down the escaped prisoner; he didn't have much hopes of his plan for the following day.

It was a short summer night, but for Matt there were far too many hours to spend thinking about young Billy. He'd let the boy down, and he could see no hope of bringing Logan in for the crime he'd surely committed. Billy was past caring, but it seemed wrong to leave a stain on his name. Besides, even a girl like Mirabelle deserved justice.

Before the first light of dawn Matt stirred up the fire and brewed coffee, waking the two cowboys. Half an hour later they made ready to leave.

'Hey, Jed, I reckon I left your knife by the fire after I cut the bacon,' Monty said, as he tied his bedroll to the back of his saddle.

'You'd lose your own ears if they wasn't held down by your hat,' Jed grumbled, tightening his cinch then going to search by the scattered ashes. With a wink at Matt, Monty ducked round to the other side of Jed's horse.

By the time Jed came back, Monty and Matt were both mounted. Jed grabbed his reins and put a foot in the iron, but as he put his weight on it, the saddle slid round under the horse's belly, landing him on his back.

Monty hooted with laughter.

'So, that was funny, huh?' Jed said equably, getting up and swiping dust off his pants. 'Was from where I'm sat,' Monty replied. 'Figured since you're so all-fired good at reading a trail you'd like a good close look at the ground before we start.'

'Not a bad idea. There's another trick or two you might want to learn about readin' a trail.'

'Yeah?' Monty sounded wary.

'Yeah. Horse shit now, that's real useful.' Jed fixed his saddle and mounted. 'Smell it, feel it, you can tell how long it's been lyin' there, so you know how far ahead your man is. Sometimes you have to get right down an' rub your nose in it. I'll show you how it's done, just as soon as we find somethin' good an' fresh. I'll see you do it real thorough.'

It was the last joke they made that day. They split up, each man following one set of hoof prints, only to find that an hour later they were back together, a couple of miles from their overnight camp.

'Do we try again?' Jed asked, taking a mouthful of water to rinse the dust from his throat.

'No.' Matt stared at the empty prairie. 'It's still my guess Rawlins will head for the mountains. We've wasted enough time trying to track him; we'll take a chance on cutting him off.' He pointed north-west. 'We ride hard and fast until we hit the foothills, then turn south. If we find tracks we follow them; if not we'll try taking the high ground and see if we can spot him.'

They made good time, pushing the horses, and before noon they reached the rising ground that had been no more than a purple haze on the horizon at daybreak. Following an old trail that ran south, they rode a few yards apart, watching for any sign that a horse had been ridden into the mountains.

The heat bore down on men and horses. The three men rode in silence as the hours passed, with mouths that were parched and eyes that ached from the unrelenting sun. Their horses stumbled on wearily, close to exhaustion. They found no tracks.

Matt finally called a halt where a couple of spindly trees cast some shade. 'He can't have come this way,' he said, wincing as he eased out of the saddle. 'Guess I got it wrong again.' He took a telescope from his saddle-bag. 'Take care of the horses then brew some coffee. I'll take a walk up the hill and see what I can make out.'

'I never seen through one of them things,' Monty said. 'You mind if I come along?'

'Coffee'll be hot when you get back.' Jed filled the coffee pot then tipped the rest of the water from the canteen into his hat, holding it for his horse to drink. 'We could sure use some more water.'

'There's a deep pool in a hollow above that shoulder of

rock,' Matt said, pointing up a nearby draw. 'Never known it run dry, even in this sort of heat, though it won't be easy to get the horses up there, ground's rough.'

'You know this territory?' Monty asked, as they started up the steep hill.

'Ran cattle here, when I was about your age,' Matt said. 'Friend of mine still has a spread a little further on. Ranch house is just out of sight thataway. Haven't seen Ches in years; he's no call to ride to Jeopardy, and I don't get out this way no more.'

The two men stood together at the top of a steep drop, staring to the east across twenty miles of prairie. In all that hard empty land they could see no sign of movement, no telltale column of dust. Matt stared long and hard at the heat-haze, than handed the telescope to Monty. 'Day's none too clear,' he said, 'but I don't reckon Rawlins is out there.'

While the cowboy exclaimed over the view through the telescope, Matt perched on a rock, thinking about his next move. He had some hard choices to make. If Coulter's men had released Rawlins, would they risk taking him back to Jeopardy and hiding him there? Maybe, with Jay Brand and Bert Dobson to back him, he could try searching the town.

'Come on,' he said at last. 'Let's go get that coffee and move on. Seeing we're sure we haven't missed him we'll keep going south. We can find a place to camp at nightfall and take another look when the air's clear in the morning.'

'And if we still don't see him?'

'We quit,' Matt said flatly.

The volley of shots broke through the silence, and the

three horses scattered, their riders cursing. They had been moving slow, watching the ground, half-comatose with the heat and the day of hard riding. The attack was so sudden they were almost jolted from their saddles as the horses leapt in alarm.

There was no time to think, no time to do anything but struggle to master their terrified mounts as a second barrage of shots followed the first, the noise adding to their confusion. For a few perilous seconds they were too stunned even to judge which way they needed to run to escape from the deadly hail of lead.

Matt's horse squealed in panic as a bullet nicked a few hairs off its ear, but the sheriff had recovered now; their attackers were holed up in the rising ground to the west of them. They'd picked their spot well; they were invisible in the shadows, with the lowering sun shining blindingly down from behind them.

Amidst the chaotic whirl of motion going on around him, Matt felt time slow down, the way it did when a man's life was on the line. He was aware of the sharp whine of lead hurtling through the air. With sudden clarity he saw dust exploding up from beneath the feet of Jed's mount, and a moment later a bullet whisked the hat off Monty's head. The cowboy cursed and wrestled to turn his horse away from the relentless assault.

'This way!' Matt yelled, driving back his heels and bending low over the saddlebow. He led the two cowboys towards the open prairie, cursing himself for a fool. Rawlins and his mysterious allies had been ahead of him at every turn, and he'd be lucky if the three of them got out of this with their lives. Reaching down to draw his rifle from its scabbard, he felt a sudden shock run up his arm as his hand touched the butt. He flinched then tried again. The polished wood was slippery beneath his fingers and the attempt sent a jolt of red-hot fire all the way to his shoulder, tearing an involuntary grunt of pain from his throat. Glancing down he saw red blood spurting from the pad of flesh below his thumb.

Beside him Monty was half turning in his saddle, the reins looped over the horn and his rifle in his hands. 'Save your lead and ride,' Matt rasped, 'they're too well hidden.'

A moment later they were safely out of range. Along the unbroken line of hills there was nothing to show where their enemies were. 'What now?' Monty asked, rubbing a hand over his head. 'Hell, I'm gonna miss that hat.'

Matt had no answer. Without more men he couldn't hope to root Rawlins out of the hills. Even one man could keep them at bay while he held the high ground, and from the blistering fire the enemy had just delivered he knew he was facing three at least.

In daylight he might try skirting round behind the gunmen, he knew the country well enough, but at night it wouldn't be easy. Besides, Rawlins and his buddies had proved they were no fools, they'd surely move on.

He couldn't outguess them, it was time to get smart. Matt slumped sideways, grabbing at the pommel as if he'd just lost his balance. He half fell out of the saddle, letting his grip loosen so he ended up on his knees in the dust.

'Hey, Sheriff, you hurt?' Jed was instantly off his horse and at his side, staring at the blood dripping from Matt's hand on to the ground.

'No, it's just a scratch. But I had an idea. If they think I'm out of action could be they'll get careless. It's been a long hot day; they won't want to move far tonight, if they don't have to. We'll try to get behind them before daybreak, that might give us the edge.' He hunched over and collapsed on to his side. 'They won't know that bullet just nicked my hand, if they've got good eyesight they'll be able to see the blood.'

'That wound needs cleaning anyways,' Monty said, leaning down from the saddle to offer his canteen to Jed. 'Reckon there's enough left in there.'

'No,' Matt said sharply, 'we'll need every drop if this is going to work. The horses have to drink and we'll have no time to look for more water.'

'You can't just leave it bleeding,' Jed protested.

'Tie my bandanna round it, but don't let them see what you're doing, we want them to think I'm dying, or close to it.'

Jed obeyed, then he and Monty watered the horses, before they took a meagre drink for themselves.

'I could ride back to that pool up in the hills,' Monty said, coming to give Matt his share. He looked back the way they'd come. 'Wouldn't take me more'n a couple of hours.'

'The sheriff said no,' Jed told him, hunkering down beside them.

Matt lay staring up at the deep blue of the sky. 'You might not get back before dark. We need to move on soon. We can manage one night without water. Give it a while though; you boys go ahead and argue if you want, make it look like you can't figure what to do.'

'Play-acting,' Monty said delightedly, 'always did have a hankering to try my hand in the thee-atre.' He rose and turned to Jed, waving a fist under his friend's nose. 'Listen here, you dumb jackass, best thing we can do is head back to the water-hole, so's the sheriff here can have some coffee, and we can clean up that there nasty wound.'

Jed shook his head. 'Nope. Matt told us there's a spread

44

a few miles south-east of here, and it belongs to a friend of his.' He pointed. 'South-east, right? Just over the next rise. We'll go there, so that wound gets tended before it goes bad.'

'Since when did you tell me what to do?' Monty demanded. 'Tell you what, I just recalled that dry creek we crossed not half an hour ago, I bet if I dig under the stones I'll find us some water.' He ran his hand over his head again. 'Hell, I feel like I'm near enough naked. Reckon I'm gonna go fetch my hat too.'

'Are you crazy?' Matt shouted, almost on his knees before he remembered he was supposed to be badly hurt. He slumped back down again. Monty was already snatching up the empty canteens and running to his horse.

'I'll be back in a couple of shakes of a maverick's tail,' the cowboy said, driving back with his heels. Soon there was nothing to see but a fast-moving cloud of dust.

'Dammit, couldn't you have stopped him?' Matt grumbled.

'Monty?' Jed shook his head. 'Never did find a way to stop him doin' what he wanted. It surely ain't that important?'

'I want them to see us leave,' Matt explained. They need to be sure we've given up. If the light goes it won't work.'

'Well, you just go on lyin' there while I give the horses some grain,' Jed said. 'Then I'll come fussin' round you like some old hen. Monty ain't the only one can do this actin' stuff.'

'Best if you just do things same as normal,' Matt advised, 'Rawlins ain't stupid.'

Barely half an hour had passed when they saw Monty returning. He came at a jog, keeping in the shadow of the hills. With a sudden whoop he clapped spurs to his horse, driving it to a gallop, heading straight for the place where they'd been ambushed. As the cowboy got close he leant down out of the saddle, hanging precariously alongside his mount's shoulder, his leg hitched over the saddle horn, his head dangerously close to the flying hoofs.

'Damn show-off,' Jed scoffed, but there was worry in his voice.

'Yaah!' With a shout of triumph Monty scooped his hat from the ground. Several shots rang from the hills. Dust flicked up from the ground yards away from the running horse, but the cowboy rode on, pressing his horse hard until he was well out of range.

As the last echo faded away Monty came back to them, grinning widely. He handed Jed three full canteens and slapping his dusty hat on his knee before putting it back on his head. 'Told you I wouldn't be long. And those shots didn't come nowhere near me.'

'You got lucky,' Matt said sombrely. 'You're a jackass, but you're a useful one. You got me some information. I was afraid they might have just left one man up there, but those shots didn't come from the same gun. All we need now is some luck, let's hope they don't move tonight.'

CHAPTER FIVE

'Did I say we needed luck?' Matt said bitterly. The stars were bright, giving them just enough light to see the rock fall barring their way. It was a vast tumble of boulders that would be difficult for a man to climb, let alone a horse.

'We could try it on foot,' Monty suggested.

'No, turn around; there's another way, though it'll take us longer.'

'Figure we only got two hours to daybreak,' Jed cautioned.

'I know it.' Matt sighed. 'But without the horses we'll have no chance of following if they get away from us. We'll go on back to that first gully, it won't be easy but I reckon we can make it.'

At first the gully was shallow and wide, but gradually it grew steeper, with rock walls closing in on either side. Their mounts stumbled over loose stone, the ground treacherous at every step.

'Jee-Hoshaphat,' Monty hissed, as his horse caught its foot between two rocks and fell. He stepped out of the saddle and away before the animal slithered downhill on its side, struggling to find a footing. Monty scrambled after it hastily, gentling the horse with hand and voice as it lay snorting, unable or unwilling to get up in such a narrow space. Jed dismounted, throwing his reins to Matt. Between them the cowboys hauled the horse around to face uphill, then set their shoulders against the animal's haunches.

'Gittup dammit,' Monty gasped, and with a great heave the horse struggled upright. It stood trembling with its head down while Monty ran his hand down its legs. 'Seems OK.'

'Maybe we'd all best walk for a while,' Matt said, easing out of the saddle. He bit down on a curse as his arm knocked against Jed's horse; his injured hand was swollen now, and when he tried to bunch the fingers into a fist the pain took his breath away.

Progress was even slower on foot, but at last they emerged from the rocky gorge and the starlight showed them a stretch of grass sloping away towards a distant peak.

'That way?' Jed asked hopefully, lifting boot to stirrup.

'For a while, but make the most of it, we'll be on foot again soon.' Matt led them at a jog, angling right. Around the shoulder of the hill they descended a little to cross a stream, dry but for a few shallow pools. The horses drank gratefully, and the men refilled their canteens, although the water tasted stale.

'Where now?' Monty asked, peering into darkness ahead.

'Up there,' Matt replied. The ravine was even narrower than the one they'd just climbed. 'Could be this one's blocked too. I'd best go on foot first, take a look see.'

Within minutes he came slithering back down to them, loose stone rattling away from his boots. 'The horses stay here,' he said briefly. 'No time to go messing around look-

48

ing for a better way up. Bring your rifles.'

As he climbed Matt was cursing silently; again the luck was with Rawlins. Ten years ago a man could ride this way, now frost and melt water had broken the rock so bad that he wasn't even sure the three of them would make it on foot. And they were running out of time.

The sky had lightened a few shades, black giving way to deep blue as they laboured slowly upwards. Matt hissed a warning as Jed's foot sent a loose rock tumbling back down the ravine. A few more minutes and they were almost at the top, and it was light enough for him to see the two cowboys' faces as he waved a warning to them. He cocked his rifle as quietly as he could and eased up a few more yards until he could see over the lip of the ravine.

There was nobody in sight. It was almost daylight, the arroyo willows near the top of the gorge already showing grey green. Unless Rawlins had moved on, he'd be over the next rise; Matt knew the spot, a rocky bowl, which had provided the perfect cover for their ambush the day before.

They moved silently across the thin mountain grass, fanning out a little, each man intent, gun at the ready, aware that if the outlaws had got wind of their coming they could be walking into a trap. The eastern sky was pale now, the sun a rim of fire on the horizon; a few minutes and it would be daylight.

Matt and the cowboys came over the crest of the hill. Not more than a dozen paces distant were three men, two already on their horses. As the third man turned in alarm, his boot in the iron ready to mount, Matt got a clear view of his face. It was Rawlins.

He would never get a better chance, and he didn't hesitate. The man was a murderer, convicted and sentenced to death. In a heartbeat Matt had the rifle up, its butt cold against his cheek. Rawlins, reaching for his rifle even as he swung into the saddle, was in his sights.

The other men were moving. One of them had a six-gun in his fist, and was thumbing back the hammer, but Matt barely noticed. Ignoring the pain in his injured hand, he tightened his grip, drawing in a breath. His finger closed on the trigger, but he'd reckoned without the swelling, which made his finger jam against the trigger guard for a fraction of a second as he squeezed, and in that instant he knew his slug would miss.

The recoil set Matt's injured hand on fire, and he bit his lip, drawing blood that tasted hot and metallic on his dry tongue. He worked the action for a second shot. Beside him he was aware of Monty firing, of Jed yelling defiance as he charged at the nearest man, who hadn't drawn a gun but was spurring his horse to get past them and escape.

Bullets spat, but where they came from or where they went Matt couldn't tell. Sobbing now, the agony in his hand shooting all the way to his shoulder, he took aim again. Rawlins was dragging his horse's head around, a dark stain spreading high on his shoulder. Matt's aim hadn't been so bad after all. The wound didn't seem to be slowing the man down any though; he put spurs to his horse, sending it leaping to a gallop.

Matt's second slug sang past Rawlins's back. The outlaw wasn't hanging around for any more. His horse was going flat out, and before Matt could fire for a third time he was over the lip of the hollow, close behind the other two men.

'Dammit to hell!' Matt exploded, hugging his tortured hand to his chest as Monty and Jed ran past him to send a couple of futile shots after the fleeing outlaws.

*

'We know he's hurt,' Monty said, bringing his horse along-side Matt's and staring up at the grass slope which stretched invitingly up into the mountains. 'We got at least eight hours to nightfall. Why don't we try tracking them?'

'Because they know we're after them,' Matt said patiently. They'd been over all this before. 'Even with twice as many men I'd think hard about going on. There's a hundred places they could hide out and wait for us. You want to commit suicide, you might as well go jump off that damn cliff.'

Monty opened his mouth to argue some more, but a look from Jed silenced him, and the three of them turned to ride slowly downhill. They rode without saying a word until they were back on the open prairie. The taste of defeat was bitter in Matt's mouth, but he wasn't prepared to risk lives needlessly; Rawlins had won, for the moment. There was small comfort in the thought that the bullet he'd stopped might still finish him if it wasn't properly tended.

'How about that friend of yours?' Monty asked, break-ing in on Matt's thoughts. 'Maybe we should try asking him for some men.'

'No, Ches Marryat doesn't carry a gun these days.' Matt said. 'And he's never had many men working for him; it's a small spread, he takes on extra hands when he needs them. Anyways, we're way outside my jurisdiction here. It's my job to take care of Jeopardy, not chase escaped convicts right across the state. I've done all I can for now.'

It was in Matt's mind that he'd maybe not be sheriff much longer, and then he could offer his help to Jay Brand. He'd take to the trail as a deputy marshal, even if

51

he had to work for no pay. Trouble was, by the time Jay's leg was mended, Rawlins could be a thousand miles away.

Matt bit down suddenly on his lip, amazed that such a small injury should hurt that bad. He hadn't said as much to Monty and Jed, but he'd have been crazy to go on; he knew he wouldn't be able to fire a gun for some days. The whole of his arm felt hot to the touch now, and his wrist was so swollen his shirt was stretched taut over the angry red flesh.

Nearly two days later they halted briefly where the trail forked; the two cowboys turned to head back to the Circle T, leaving Matt to ride the last few miles into Jeopardy alone.

'Thanks for your time, boys,' Matt said. 'Next time you come into town you'd better call in and fetch your pay. Tell Will I'm grateful. You did all you could; no fault of yours Rawlins is still out there.' He swiped a few drops of sweat from his forehead and straightened in the saddle as the prairie shimmered slightly in front of him. For a second he had been in danger of falling.

'Our pleasure,' Jed said easily, letting his horse turn for home.

'Sure, nothing we like better than riding in all this heat an' dust,' Monty agreed, curbing his horse as it tried to follow Jed's mount. 'One thing though, Sheriff, seeing you and me's friends now. Twice you've managed to lay me out when I've been having me a little fun in the Blue Diamond. How d'you do that?'

'My secret,' Matt replied, hauling in a deep breath and trying to keep his mind straight. He grinned. 'Sorry, son. The day you sign the pledge, that's the day I'll tell you. Say howdy to those two young hooligans of Will's for me, and tell Mrs Trent I sure hope she's feeling better.'

'I'll do that.' Monty touched a finger to his hat and loosed his hold on the rein, letting his horse take off after Jed's.

Matt rode back to Jeopardy slowly. His mind was racing feverishly; conjuring up all sorts of crazy ideas. He almost convinced himself that Rawlins was hiding out in town. Slumping in the saddle, Matt found himself making a hopeless search through Jeopardy's streets, then a moment later he was high in the mountains, where eagles came swooping down to squabble over Monty Caine's hat. At last one bird came to tear gobbets of flesh from Matt's bleeding arm, and with a gasp of pain he came awake, swaying as his horse plodded homewards.

The street was deserted in the midday heat. Matt dismounted wearily outside his cabin, staggering a little as his feet hit the ground. It needed no thought to remove saddle and bridle; the horse would find its own way to the water trough and its place in the barn; he'd send Two Shots to rub it down.

He was vaguely surprised to see the door to his cabin was closed; Jay Brand would be stifling in there. Shaking his head Matt knew the marshal wasn't that crazy, he must be someplace else. Perhaps he'd finally persuaded Doc Gardino to get him a pair of crutches. Matt walked past the door and headed for his office; he'd feel better once he'd had a cup of coffee, and Two Shots was sure to have a pot boiling on the stove.

The office door didn't yield under Matt's hand. It was locked. This didn't seem to make much sense, and for a second Matt wondered if this was another of his crazy dreams. He searched clumsily under the sidewalk for the stone that hid the key, awkwardly left-handed because of the bandage tied around his right. He let himself in, cursing as a wave of hot stale air hit him. Despite the heat, the stove was cold. Where the hell was Two Shots? Probably drunk or sleeping it off. Matt staggered outside again to look in the ramshackle lean-to. It was empty.

Back in his office Matt was suddenly dizzy. He sank into his chair and let his eyes close, though that didn't shut out the images thundering through his brain. They wouldn't leave him be. Billy fell from the roof, screaming words he'd never been able to voice when he was alive, and Mirabelle rose, dripping and bloody from her bed, her red painted lips smiling.

Lurching to his feet, Matt made for the open door. He was dripping with perspiration yet shivering as if he'd been dunked in icy water. Maybe a drink would help. When he stepped out through the open door there were men waiting for him. Logan and Mendez he knew. Behind them was a bearded man he didn't recognize, six foot, and almost as broad as he was high.

'Something I can do for you?' Matt dropped his hand to his gun, but it was a useless gesture, he could no longer fit his swollen fingers around the butt. His saddle was on the sidewalk, and he reached down left handed to lift his rifle from its holster.

'That's what I was about to say,' Logan replied, hitching his thumbs into his belt. 'I was wondering what business you had in my office.'

'Maybe he was figurin' to steal somethin',' the bearded man said. 'You reckon that rifle's yours, Logan?'

'Could be.' Logan's lips curled in an unpleasant smile. 'Well, Turner, you got anythin' to say? In case you ain't got the message yet, I'm the law around here now.'

'You've got him worried, Logan,' Mendez said, chuckling. 'Look at him. He's sweatin' like a pig.'

Matt met Logan's eyes, fighting the waves of dizziness that were sweeping through him. 'I've got nothing to say to you, Logan. Be obliged if you'd get out of my way.'

'Why sure.' Logan stepped aside, his small eyes hard. Matt went to pass him, but he was suddenly jolted to a halt as Mendez's arm shot out and clamped around his neck. The bearded man reached to take the rifle, then lifted Matt's six-gun from its holster. Once Matt was unarmed Mendez changed his grip, one hand clamping on each of Matt's upper arms.

The street swayed alarmingly, and jagged red light flashed across Matt's vision.

Logan reached out and took a handful of his shirtfront. 'Well, Mr Turner, can't say I'm surprised you didn't bring Rawlins back with you,' he said. 'But then, you had most of these townsfolks fooled; they didn't know it was you let him go in the first place. Sure will surprise them when you come up for trial.'

'Don't reckon they'll be surprised at anything you and Duke Coulter dream up,' Matt replied through gritted teeth, concentrating hard to keep from passing out. Mendez's fingers squeezed his swollen arm and pain stabbed through him. 'They must know they'll see no justice done in Jeopardy while he's around. But I think you're forgetting something: Jay Brand's a federal marshal, could be he'll have something to say about this. Not to mention I've got two witnesses who saw me shoot Rawlins.'

Logan's eyes narrowed. 'I heard them cowpokes from the Trent spread rode with you. But I don't think they'll give us any trouble. They'll be movin' on real soon, lookin' for work. Duke'll see to that. As for Brand, him an' the other one lit out two days ago. Right after I got me elected as Jeopardy's new sheriff.'

'Sheriff? You?' Matt's head was spinning, his arm hurting so much he almost felt he'd be grateful if Mendez yanked it off at the shoulder. He began to laugh then, wild hysterical guffaws which took his breath away.

Logan's face loomed at him, strangely distorted. Then in the place of the skinny features, Matt saw a white knuckled fist. He was past even trying to dodge. The blow hit him square on the jaw and the world turned red, then grey. He was aware of the boards tilting beneath his feet before the blackness closed in, but he didn't feel a thing as his head crunched down on the sidewalk.

CHAPTER SIX

'You won't need to worry about Turner no more, Duke.'

'Whatever you're planning, try to be discreet,' Coulter said drily, 'there are still a few men in this town with influence. I have my reputation to think of.'

Somebody laughed. 'Sure, boss, if you say so. But pretty soon the whole of Jeopardy's gonna be sittin' right in your pocket.'

Through a haze of confusion and a persistent drumming pain in his skull, Matt tried to make sense of the words. He opened his eyes and found himself staring at a pair of travel-stained boots.

'Shame the river's low. Be real easy to get rid of him that way, an' nobody would ever know.'

'We can wait till it's dark, cart him out and bury him someplace.'

Logan. Matt's fevered brain was working now. Logan and Duke, and at least two more men. They were talking about killing him. There didn't seem to be much he could do about it. His jaw ached ferociously, and his head was pounding. Trying to form a fist he found he couldn't move any of his fingers. Even that didn't seem to matter much, though he had an idea it wasn't good news.

Some corner of his mind protested. Was he going to let the likes of Duke Coulter beat him? Trouble was, if he tried to fight his way out they only had to hit his injured arm to reduce him to a helpless wreck. And he was so tired. It would be so easy to let his eyes drift shut again and lapse back into the dark.

From somewhere a memory emerged. Logan again. And Duke. Too old. They'd said he was too old to be sheriff. Could be they were right, but the thought was enough to stiffen his backbone. Matt Turner wasn't ready to quit just yet, at least, not if it meant Logan taking his place.

He had to move. Somehow. He had one useless arm and he was burning up with fever, but any second now the men crowded into his office would realize he was conscious and any tiny advantage he had would be gone. Very slowly he flexed his left hand into a fist. Not good, he'd always been right-handed. Even the trick he'd used on Monty a couple of times wouldn't serve him here, not with three or four of them to deal with. He needed a gun.

If only his head was clear. It buzzed, full of sounds and images caused by the fever, more vivid that reality. These men were planning his death; he probably should have been scared, or angry at least, but he could barely get his mind to function.

Fuzzily, Matt noticed Logan's handgun in its holster not far above him. To reach it he would need to be standing, or at least on his knees. Sunlight streamed in through the window; it was still only mid-afternoon. They'd see him as soon as he made his move. There was the rifle rack behind him, but he had no hope of getting that far.

Fighting the desire to simply close his eyes and forget the whole thing, Matt tested his leg muscles, tensing them, trying to send his body clear messages through the fever muddling his head. He figured how it had to work. Kneeling would do. Logan wore his gun on the left, that was a help, but only as long as he kept facing away from Matt.

Although he knew it was a hopeless gesture, Matt rolled, lurched, rose to his knees and made a left-handed grab for Logan's gun. Somebody shouted a warning, even as his hand closed on the six-gun's butt and dragged it from the holster.

There was a moment when the room seemed frozen, no sound, no movement. The gun was almost in his grasp, beneath thumb and finger. Trouble was, getting that far had robbed Matt of his last reserve of strength. Across the room Mendez was drawing his Colt, an evil grin on his face. And until that moment Matt hadn't noticed that the bearded man was holding a shotgun. Pointing his way.

Matt stared down the deadly black barrel. This was it then. At such close range at least he wouldn't have time to feel much.

A deafening crash shattered the silence. Matt clenched his jaw, determined not to flinch, but there was no searing blast of shot. Several men came bursting in through the door, the first of them having thrown it open so violently that the glass had erupted from its frame to fall jingling to the floor.

Time started up again, and the room was filled with noise, with people. Matt slid to the floor once more, drifting back into the nightmarish haze of his fever. Somebody grabbed him by the shoulders.

'Matt. You OK?'

A familiar face was staring into his.

'Doc?' Matt's voice echoed strangely in his own ears, as if he were shouting down a barrel.

'Well, looks like we were just in time.' Will Trent stood

blocking the light from the doorway, right on the heels of Doc Gardino and Kurt Jensen. Grant Pechey from the train depot was peering over Trent's shoulder.

'We were about to send for you, Doctor,' Duke Coulter said smoothly. 'Turner's gone crazy. I guess it's not his fault, he's burning up with fever, but he was threatening to shoot me.'

'Is that so?'

'He took my gun,' Logan growled. 'Hell, I didn't know he was mad enough to try a stunt like that.'

'He's not mad, just sick,' Doc Gardino said, gently taking the six-gun from Matt's limp grasp. 'Here, you'd better take care of this, Sheriff. Come on, Matt.' He took hold of Matt's left hand to pull him upright.

Kurt Jensen came around as if to take hold of Matt's right arm. 'Don't,' Matt croaked urgently. He couldn't deal with that much pain just now. 'I can manage.'

'I guess you must have Matt's gun somewhere, Logan.' Will Trent kept his tone even, peaceable. 'It doesn't seem to be in his holster.'

'I took it away from him. In case he hurt somebody.'

'That's reasonable,' Trent said. 'But you can give it to me now, I'll look after it until he's better.'

Next minute they were out of the office. Leaning on Doc Gardino's arm, Matt made it as far as the steps, then his legs folded beneath him. He fell against the hitching rail, pain lanced through his hand and jagged bolts of lightning flashed through his head. The world folded in upon itself and once again everything disappeared.

There was a rough timber roof only a foot above his eyes. Thin shafts of sunlight were coming in from somewhere. Matt tried to turn towards the light and groaned as the movement set a drum throbbing in his head. His hand hurt too. He peered at it in the uncertain light, and saw that the swollen flesh was covered with a clean white bandage.

A moment later a face appeared at his side. 'Hey, you're awake!' It was Kurt Jensen, his lined features creased into a smile. 'Sure is good to see you, Matt. Reckon for a while there we didn't think you'd make it.'

'Why. . . ?' His voice was a croak, his throat so dry it was agony to swallow.

'Hold on.' Kurt vanished, returning swiftly to hold a cup of water to Matt's lips.

Matt drank thirstily. 'Thanks. What am I doing in your roof?'

'Keeping out of sight. Coulter's men have been looking for you.'

'Coulter?' Matt asked vaguely.

'Yeah. We thought we'd got 'em fooled. The night after we came and fetched you out of the office, Grant stopped a freight train just outside of town and a few of us rode down there in a bunch, like we had something to hide. At the same time we sent a wagon out on the eastbound road, figuring they'd work out that was the decoy and we'd put you on the train. Either way, we reckoned they wouldn't be looking for you in Jeopardy. Worked real well. Only yesterday they started searching the town. That snake Logan must've checked with the railroad, and figured out you never went that way. They were here a couple of hours ago, poking around, but they never thought to climb up here.'

'Can't say I'm surprised,' Matt mumbled, knocking his knee hard on the roof as he tried to turn over.

'Take it easy, I'll get word to the Doc. We're planning to

61

get you out of here, sooner the better.'

It wasn't Doc Gardino who came, but Will Trent. Matt heard him exchange words with Kurt about some work the blacksmith was doing. 'I was hoping you'd be finished before dark,' Will said loudly, his voice carrying easily to where Matt lay, 'didn't plan on staying in town tonight.'

'Should be a moon,' Kurt offered. 'Up to you when you take it, job'll be done in three hours. Got a horse to shoe, then I'll get right on that last piece.'

Matt peered down through a gap between the planks. He could see the rancher, standing in the doorway. Beyond him, leaning on the hitching rail, was one of Coulter's men, holding the rein of a flea-bitten grey mare.

'Guess that'll have to do,' Will said. 'I'll bring the wagon over now, can't leave it in front of Joe's store all day.'

'Drive it round back,' Kurt replied, 'be easier to load.'

Careful to make no sound, Matt slid even further into the narrow roof space, so he could see out behind the blacksmith's shop. He watched Trent bring the wagon and water his horses, then walk away towards the hotel. Below him Coulter's man sat smoking a cigar, watching Kurt hammer a horseshoe into shape.

Time dragged by. The man with the grey mare left. A couple of times Kurt walked out to the wagon, loading the parts for Trent's new windmill. Once he crawled under the wagon's seat, pushing a couple of pieces of wood in front of him.

Later, Matt moved again, and found a crack in the roof that allowed him to see the back of the Blue Diamond saloon. He saw Sally Schott, a robe over her faded chemise, slouching across to an outhouse, a whiskey bottle only half hidden under her arm. Half an hour later she came back, weaving a little.

Darkness fell. Matt dozed, the sound of the bellows and Kurt's hammer loud and jarring in his dreams. Then the sounds stopped and he woke suddenly. There was movement below, two horsemen riding into Jeopardy, coming not from the road but across open country, barely visible in the first silver glow of moonrise. The riders dismounted by the saloon's back door, one of them awkward because he had an arm in a sling. As the man entered the saloon he swept his hat off, and in the light that flooded out of the door Matt saw him clearly: it was Harve Rawlins.

'Kurt!' Matt bellowed, ignoring the hurt to his hand as he slithered swiftly to the gap where the blacksmith had climbed up earlier.

'Hush up,' Kurt Jensen said, craning his neck to stare back at him. 'You want to get yourself killed? It's not time to go yet.'

'I just saw Rawlins. He's over in the Blue Diamond right now.'

'And exactly what were you thinking of doing about that? Maybe you figure you'll just walk in there and arrest him, right under Duke's nose, huh? Or perhaps you want me to fetch Grant and the Doc, and we'll make up a posse? You ain't wearing a badge no more, Matt. Just pipe down, and wait for Will to get back here.'

'Rawlins is a murderer.' Matt ground out the words, chewing on his anger.

'Just like Logan,' Kurt said bleakly. 'It was him killed that girl, and he got young Billy shot. The whole town knows it. But right now you're not fit to take on a kid, Matt, let alone half-a-dozen men. Here's Doc, we'll get you down from there.'

'Some doctor you are,' Matt growled a few minutes later, sitting on Kurt's anvil. 'Kurt tells me I've been here four days, and I still can't use this arm right.'

'You're damn lucky you've got an arm,' Gardino replied, deftly unwrapping the bandage. 'You should be thanking me for working miracles. Was a time I thought I'd have to take it off, clear up to the shoulder. Poison was working its way into that fool head of yours too, that's why you were out of your senses. You can rest up at Will's place, get your strength back. I visited Martha yesterday, she'll keep an eye on this till it's healed.'

'I can do that for myself,' Matt said fretfully.

'Oh sure,' the doctor replied, 'the way you looked after it in the first place. Get yourself some sense, Matt, and do as you're told for once. Me and the rest of your friends here in Jeopardy didn't save your life just so you could throw it away.'

The wagon, heavily loaded, pulled slowly out on to the road. A half moon showed the way, once the lights of Jeopardy were left behind.

'Hold it!' They were nearly out of town. A horseman carrying a flaming torch suddenly erupted from behind the grain store, which stood alone beyond the empty train yard. He was a big man, his bearded face taking on a sinister look in the wavering torch light. When Will didn't pull up he rode out in front of the team.

Will cursed as he got the beasts under control. 'If you're planning a hold up you've got the wrong man, mister. I got nothing here that's worth a cent to anyone but me. Don't even have the price of a drink in my pocket.'

'I'm here to take a look in your wagon,' the man said. 'Light down.'

'You've got no right—'

A second rider came to join the first. 'You got us all

64

wrong, Trent. Zeke's a town deputy, all sworn in official, three days ago. This here's a matter of upholding the law.'

'Logan.' The rancher spat into the dust when he recognized the newcomer. 'What are you talking about?'

'We're looking for a murderer. The man who got busted out of jail when Matt Turner was the law around here.'

'Rawlins? My boys were out in the mountains with Matt when the sheriff winged him. There's no reason he'd be hiding out in Jeopardy.'

'No reason except that our one-time sheriff turned him loose in the first place.'

'That's the craziest thing I ever heard. Anyway, I'm not carrying any murderer. There's nobody on this wagon but me, reckon you can see that.' Will clucked to his horses to move on, but Logan reached down and grabbed at the reins.

'We're searching this wagon, with or without your say so, Trent.'

'Fine, if that's what you want. But don't go messing with my load, it's real heavy, I don't want it shifting when I'm halfway across the river.'

'Here.' The man called Zeke thrust the torch into Will's hands. 'Hold that.' He got down from his horse and dragged the cover off the heavily laden wagon. 'Can't see if there's anything under all this stuff,' he said, and before either Will or Logan could stop him he drew his six-gun and fired a shot into the centre of the load. The bullet hit metal with a sharp clang then ricocheted into the dark, narrowly missing Logan's head. Logan gave a small yelp of surprise then turned on the man, cursing long and loud.

Will Trent laughed. 'You better be careful, Zeke, a man can get himself hanged for killing a lawman.'

'Well, leastways we know there's nobody in there,' Zeke said.

'How d'you work that out?' Logan growled.

'He woulda yelled, the way you did. An' Trent here wasn't worried; don't reckon he'd be laughin' if a friend of his was hidden in there. Wouldn't do no harm to make sure, though.' He pointed the gun, his knuckles whitening as he began to squeeze the trigger.

'Don't!' Logan yelled. 'Damn fool, the next shot might kill one of us! All right, Trent, you can go. Duke said to remind you about that meetin' he wants to fix up. You better come callin' real soon.'

'I'll come when I'm good and ready.' The rancher jumped down from his seat, handed the torch to Logan and picked up the tarpaulin from the ground. 'You plan to help put this back on?'

Neither man answered, turning to ride back to town, leaving him alone there in the dark. A few minutes later Will drove on, slowing the team to a walk when he reached the river, driving cautiously through the six inches of water that flowed sluggishly through the centre channel. On the far side he clucked at the team and they put their weight into their job, dragging the heavy load up the bank and into a narrow draw that would be head high in water when the floods came. Will Trent drew up among the cover of some rocks, tied the reins around the brake and climbed down.

'Hope you ain't too wet down there?' He knelt to reach under the wagon and loosed the rope behind the front axle. The plank Kurt had fixed there tilted, and Matt rolled out of his precarious hiding place, his injured hand carefully cradled against his chest.

'River was no problem,' Matt groaned, 'but this wagon could do with some springs. You damn near shook the teeth clear out of my head.'

CHAPTER SEVEN

The long night spent in the jolting wagon had left Matt weak as a new-born colt. He lay helpless in the Trents' bunkhouse for two full days, growling peevishly at anyone who came near him.

By the third day his head had stopped pounding. His thumb and fingers were finally shrinking back to their proper size, which Martha Trent claimed was thanks to a potion she had given him. Along with the medicine, rest and good food had worked their magic on Matt's body and he was beginning to feel stronger, but his mind was another matter. Whenever he wasn't asleep he spent his time fretting.

The words the doctor had said that last day kept spinning through Matt's head, almost as if the fever had returned. His friends hadn't saved his life just so he could throw it away. They wanted him to get their town back. But just how did they expect him to do it? One man wouldn't stand a chance against Logan and the rest of Coulter's hired guns.

All his life Matt had paid his dues, he'd never cared to be indebted to anyone, but he owed the folks he'd left behind far more than he could give. He couldn't recall a time when he'd felt so helpless. He thumped his good hand against the wall in frustration; he was just one man, and he was getting old. Fumbling with his right hand, still a little clumsy, he touched the holes in his vest left by the pin of the badge he'd worn for so many years. He no longer had the force of the law behind him.

Trouble was, he couldn't do the job alone, and anyone helping him would be tangling with men who made their living with the gun, men who didn't think twice about shooting to kill. Many of the townsfolk would support him, but they had a whole lot more to lose than he did. There had to be an answer. As long as Duke Coulter was in control of the town and its gun-slinging sheriff, there would be no justice in Jeopardy.

Wearily Matt's thoughts circled around. He came to no sure answers but he made up his mind to one thing: until his hand healed he had to get away, away from Jeopardy and the men who ruled the town so ruthlessly, and away from his friends so he didn't bring more violence down on their heads.

'I brought you some coffee,' Martha said, coming to his side carrying a cup. 'And one last dose of medicine.'

'You sure I need it?' Matt asked, screwing up his nose. The liquid smelt bad and tasted worse.

'Yes. I got that receipt from my half-Sioux grandmother, and you can't deny it's worked pretty well.'

'Guess that's so,' Matt replied, swallowing some of the concoction with a shudder. He heaved himself off the bunk. 'I'm feeling a whole lot better, and I'm real sorry I've been a trouble to you, Martha.'

'It's no trouble, not when I've already got Will and the boys to take care of, not to mention Monty and Jed.' She sat to watch him drink, a pale, thin woman with the marks of a long illness etched on her face. 'You're welcome here, Matt, just as long as you need to stay.'

'That's kind, but I'll be leaving, soon as I'm fit to ride.'

She nodded, and he thought she looked relieved. 'If that's what you want. We've got your horse here, Two Shots brought him. He's out in the far corral getting fat.'

There were sounds of hoofs outside, and Monty's voice shouting something, sharp in the evening air, though they couldn't hear what he said. Jed laughed and made some reply.

Martha gave a wan smile and for a second it was possible to see the pretty woman she'd been before the illness began to drain the life from her. 'Those cowboys. Sure would be good to be young and carefree that way.' She rose. 'If you're feeling better why not come over to the house? Be nice to have company at dinner.'

Matt followed the woman outside where Monty and Jed were tending their horses. 'Figured the boss would beat us back,' Monty said, opening the gate to the corral.

'Where did he go?' Martha asked. 'He didn't say anything about being late.'

'Said he had something to do,' Jed replied. 'He was headed for the south pasture.'

'You don't think he went to town?' The woman looked worried.

'Don't reckon so,' Monty said, keeping hold of his horse's reins. 'You want us to go look for him?'

'No, I guess he'll be right along. Coffee's hot. I'll bring some out while you boys wash up.'

There was a loud crash from the barn, and a moment later a small fair-haired boy came tumbling out of the door, closely followed by a slightly larger dark one who leapt on him, fists flailing. Both were covered with dust

69

from head to foot.

Momentarily triumphant, the older boy yanked his opponent roughly to his feet and dragged him across the yard. 'Where's Pa? Ricky's got somethin' to tell him.'

'It wasn't me, Ma!' Ricky bunched his fists and swung a punch at his brother's head. 'Roy's bigger; the ladder must've broke before I—'

'Quiet, the pair of you!' Martha snapped. 'you'll both get a tanning if you're not cleaned up and friends again by the time your father gets home.'

But their father didn't come home. Tight-lipped, his wife served the meal. Her sons sat quiet, their enmity forgotten, sensing something was wrong. Matt kept up a fitful conversation with the two cowboys, but it was a relief when the meal was finished. While the men sat over their coffee Martha sent the youngsters to their beds.

'I can fix the ladder, Ma,' Roy said, turning in the doorway, a little crease of worry between his brows.

She nodded. 'Sure you can. Don't fret, we'll sort it out in the morning.'

When the tall clock in the corner struck nine Monty pushed back his chair. 'Guess me an' Jed best take a ride.'

'Where will you go?' Martha asked bleakly.

'South pasture. Moon'll be up by the time we get there. That's if we don't meet the boss on the way. Don't you go worrying, Mrs Trent, it's likely his horse pulled up lame.'

'Yeah, be a long walk back,' Jed agreed. 'We'll take a spare mount.'

Once they'd gone Martha sat back down at the table opposite Matt. 'You say you're planning to move on?'

'Soon as I'm able,' Matt replied. 'I don't want to bring trouble to you Martha, you and Will have enough to deal with.'

70

There was silence for a while, each of them busy with their own thoughts, yet somehow thinking in the same direction.

'It's not that I don't want him to help you,' Martha said suddenly. 'Lord knows you've done plenty for us over the years. But anyone who stands against Coulter is going to get hurt. All your friends in Jeopardy are going to be feeling the same, Matt. We had good lives here, we thought all the fighting was over and done.'

He sighed. 'Me too. Fact is, I was about ready to hang up my gun. But it sure sticks in my craw to let Coulter and Logan take over my town.' He reached over to pat her hand. 'Don't go worrying. I'm not asking Will to get caught up in a showdown. In a couple of days I'll be gone. All you folks have to do is keep your heads down for a while.'

'You're sure he didn't go into town?' Matt looked up at Jed's dust-covered face. The cowboy's eyes were dark-shadowed and shot with red; two sleepless nights had drawn new lines around his nose and mouth.

'Don't reckon so. We asked just about everybody. Somebody would've seen him.' Jed climbed wearily from the saddle. 'I'll take a fresh horse. Monty's riding up Fire Creek, and I said I'd work from the north and meet him. Trouble is, there's just too many damn places to look.'

It had been nearly three days, and it was just as if Will Trent and his horse had vanished off the face of the earth.

'I'm done sitting around doing nothing,' Matt said suddenly. 'How about Eagle Bluff, did either of you try there?'

'It ain't exactly close to where we left him,' Jed replied, 'hut it's worth a try. You sure you're fit?'

71

'I feel better than you look.' Matt put his fingers to his mouth and whistled, and his powerful short-coupled bay came fast across the corral, slithering to a snorting halt at his side.

The two Trent boys came from back of the house, bickering as usual. Roy, the older, brushed his brother aside when he saw Matt putting on his horse's bridle.

'Are you going to look for Pa?' he asked.

'Yeah. How about you go fetch my saddle? Ricky, can you do this buckle? It's awkward one-handed, my fingers haven't quite got their strength back yet.'

Before Matt was mounted Jed was away, chomping on a hunk of bread and jerky as he rode. He turned back briefly, swallowing a mouthful in haste. 'Signal's three shots if you find anything,' he said.

Matt nodded his understanding and gestured to Roy to help him tighten the cinch.

'Can I come with you?' the boy said.

'You asked that when Monty and Jed rode out yesterday, and the day before,' Matt replied. 'You know your ma said no. What sort of cowboy are you?' he went on, seeing that the youngster was ready to argue, 'You gonna let that horse of Jeff's stand there with the sweat still on him?' He lifted into the saddle.

'I know it's hard, son,' Matt said, as the boy's head drooped, 'but your ma needs you right now. Fetch her some more water: she finds that bucket real heavy.' He tucked his right hand into the front of his vest and hauled the horse around with his left. The bay let loose with a squeal and kicked up its heels.

'Quit that,' Matt ordered, but if the circumstances had been different he'd have had a grin on his face; it felt good to be in the saddle again; he'd spent far too long lying on his back. He set the bay to a steady lope, scanning the landscape as he rode. Eagle Bluff lay about seven miles to the north. A narrow trail ran along the top, a short cut to the road that ran east to Dewsburg. It wasn't much used, seeing that the rock-face was unstable; a wrong step could send horse and rider plunging 200 feet down a sheer cliff. There was no reason for Will to have gone that way, yet Matt had a bad feeling about the place.

By the time the land began to rise towards the top of the bluff Matt was weary, every part of him aching. He slowed his horse to a walk, hooked the reins around the saddle bow and took out his canteen.

'Easy,' he cautioned, as the bay tried to hurry into a jog. 'That's one big drop up ahead, boy.' He turned left to follow the faint path along the top of the bluff. From here he had a view over mile upon mile of open prairie. Matt wished he had his telescope, but it was back in his office. Something twisted inside him. Logan's office.

The bay suddenly skittered sideways, as a buzzard rose from below and wheeled overhead, its plaintive cry loud in the silence. Matt quieted the horse and dismounted, worms squirming in his gut. Carefully he crawled to the crumbling edge of the bluff and looked over.

After three days there wasn't much left of the horse but skin and bone; the coyotes and birds had fed well. The saddle was still intact though, with Will's rifle sticking up at an angle from its boot.

There was no sign of Will Trent. Matt stood up, fumbling awkwardly for his gun. He fired off three shots, then hurried back to his horse; there was no short way off Eagle Bluff, except a suicidal jump straight down.

The ridge of land sloped away beneath the bay's hoofs, the ground rocky and treacherous with cracks waiting to trap the unwary. Even at a steady lope Matt's horse was struggling to keep its footing. At last they were down to the prairie and Matt turned to follow the base of the bluff. He rode hard now there was level ground beneath him, pushing his horse until it was flat out and ignoring the protests of muscles grown flabby from their enforced idleness. If there was any chance, no matter how small, of finding Will alive, he mustn't waste a moment.

That ride seemed endless. Matt kept his eyes open for any sign of Will, though he knew there wasn't much chance he'd survived that fall. But his body hadn't been beside the horse so there had to be some hope. Matt's heart lurched as he saw the carcass, dark against the lowering sun. It seemed that something moved, that maybe a figure was bending over the heap of bones. Then, with a cry of alarm at his approach, the bird flew up, and all was still again.

Matt stared briefly down at what remained of the horse, glad to convince himself that there was nothing human mixed with the pathetic heap of bones. His gaze roved over the base of the cliff. Will had to be here, but he could see no sign. He studied the ground, looking for tracks, then turned to look across the prairie, wondering if somebody else could have come this way. Was there a chance the rancher had been found alive, that some drifter had come to his aid?

It was hardly a sound, less than the whisper of sand brushed by the bay's hoof, but Matt whipped round, the hairs on the back of his neck prickling. The horse too had sensed something, and it shifted restlessly beneath him. Quieting the animal, Matt lit down and strode towards the dark slit in the base of the bluff.

The space looked far too narrow for a man to crawl

into, but, as he got close, Matt realized that was an illusion; a splinter of rock stood out from the cliff wall. Will Trent lay behind it, eyes staring up at the brightness of the sky, his face barely recognizable. His right eye was swollen shut, and the cheek and jaw below were misshapen and bruised black. At a glance Matt took in the fact that the man's right shoulder was shattered. It must have been hell getting himself this far, but at some point he'd had the sense to realize he needed to get out of the sun. And by doing that he'd put himself out of reach of the scavengers feasting off his horse.

In the crook of his left arm Trent cradled an empty canteen. There were teeth marks around the top. As he dropped to his knees beside his friend's body Matt could see why. Will's left hand was a mess of dried blood, three of his fingers almost torn off.

'Dear Lord,' Matt breathed.

Unbelievably, Will's left eye swivelled and focused on Matt's face. His mouth opened but no sound emerged. Matt ran to fetch his own canteen and held it to the parched lips. Will Trent swallowed eagerly, but a moment later he convulsed, groaning with pain. A trickle of bloody water ran from the corner of his mouth. 'Busted up inside,' he whispered.

'Take it easy,' Matt said, cradling the man's head. 'We'll get you home. The boys'll be along real soon. Here, just moisten your mouth some more.'

Will obeyed, keeping the water in his mouth for a moment before letting it run out down his chin.

'What happened?' Matt asked urgently. 'Did you fall?'

There was a slight shake of the head, an urgency in the sunken eye.

'Logan?' Matt hazarded.

A nod. 'Four of them. Chased me . . .'

'Along the top of the bluff?'

'They shot my horse. Guess they thought they'd killed me . . .' The words tailed off into a moan.

Rage surged through Matt. He should have found a way to bring Logan to justice when Mirabelle was murdered, but he'd let the man walk free. First Billy had died. Now Will. He should have handed his badge in a year ago and put the town in safer hands. A few years back a man like Coulter would never have got a stranglehold on Jeopardy.

But Matt's guilt was tempered with a new determination. Whatever it took, his friend's life must be avenged. Somehow. A faint sound brought his attention back to the dying man.

'Martha . . .'

'Don't worry. She'll be taken care of.'

Something that was almost a smile flickered across the battered face. 'She's dying,' Will said clearly. 'Never thought I'd go first. Tell her I'll be waiting for her, God willing . . . Look after my boys, Matt. That ranch is all they'll have. . . .'

'I'll see to it, Will, I swear.'

Will Trent gave a sigh. The life was draining from him. 'Duke wants . . .' A rattle sounded in his throat, and the solitary bloodshot eye staring up at Matt was suddenly empty of life.

CHAPTER EIGHT

'You sure he didn't say what happened?' Monty stood scowling down at Will Trent's body.

Matt looked the cowboy right in the eyes and told a barefaced lie. 'Talked about Martha and the boys,' he said, 'that was it.'

'There should be tracks,' Jed put in suddenly. He squinted up at the bluff. 'Won't take long to ride up and take a look.'

'Tomorrow,' Matt said wearily; by then maybe he'd think of a way to stop them heading into town to confront Coulter's men. If he didn't, their lives wouldn't be worth a dime, and just now he couldn't stand the thought of any more spilt blood on his conscience. 'Will's body has to be taken home, and I can't drive too good one-handed. One of you boys will have to go fetch the wagon.'

'If I do that while Jed takes a look-see up on the bluff—' Monty began.

'I said tomorrow!' Matt roared. 'Show the man some respect. I'm riding back to tell Martha. You want to leave him here alone? Best wrap him up some before he stiffens, it'll take a while to get him back to the ranch.'

'He's right, Monty,' Jed said sombrely, fetching the

bedroll from behind his saddle. 'If this wasn't no accident we'll find out soon enough.' He met Matt's eyes. 'And if Coulter's behind it we ain't gonna let it rest.'

'No,' Matt agreed, 'but if that's so then we'll deal with it. By the rule of law.'

'What law?' Monty asked bitterly. 'Jeopardy don't have no law, only Logan.'

'I said we'll deal with it. Come on, let's move.' He bent down and gently closed the dead man's staring eye. 'Might be a kindness to Mrs Trent to wash his face and put something over the worst of that mess.'

'I'll do that.' Monty eased the empty canteen away from the dead man's hold. 'You go, make the most of the daylight.'

The two men rode in silence for a while. The sun blazed its way towards the horizon, shooting brilliant bolts of red and orange across the sky.

'What else did he say?' Jed asked at last, as the ranch house came in sight, lamplight showing in the windows.

'What?' Matt had been deep in dark thoughts.

'Mr Trent said something more,' Jed persisted. 'Reckon you figured Monty's so all-fired hot-headed he'd do something stupid.'

'That's a fact. But there wasn't anything more. Maybe Will's horse got spooked by a rattlesnake or a bear, who knows.'

Martha stood at the door of the house, her hands wringing at her apron. 'You found him,' she said bleakly, as Matt dismounted and came to her side.

'I took a look at the boys,' Matt said. 'They're asleep. Reckon Roy grew up real fast today.'

Martha sat by the stove, staring at nothing. Her

husband's body was laid out in the parlour in his Sunday best, the battered face covered with clean linen. In a few hours, when there was light enough, they would bury him.

'Will told you I'm dying,' the woman said tonelessly. 'The whole town must have guessed it. I shan't see another summer. We thought Ricky and Roy would find it hard, but they'd have Will. Neither of us ever imagined . . .'

Matt said nothing. He was still filled with a bitter rage, and only some of it was directed at Duke Coulter. The rest was headed his own way. It had been cowardice, letting himself be railroaded out of Jeopardy. He should have found a way to stand up to Coulter before the man surrounded himself with hired guns. He should have arrested Logan for the murder of the girl at the Blue Diamond. It was his fault the boys were fatherless.

'Neither me or Will have any family left,' Martha went on, turning the screw on Matt with every word. 'Roy's only just turned twelve. With things in Jeopardy being the way they are, I don't see how to keep this land for him.'

'If you've got all the papers . . .'

'Duke Coulter was already trying to get his hands on the south pasture,' Martha said.

'Coulter was?' Matt was astounded. 'I didn't know that. Ever since he got here he's been buying up property in town, but what would he want with a parcel of land out here?'

'It's something to do with the railroad. The stockyard in town is too small, but it would be a real good place to build a hotel. That could make somebody a lot of money, the way folks keep moving out here. They'd need a new place to load the cattle.'

'So that's it!' Coulter's connection with Roper, the railroad manager, finally made sense. 'It could be the biggest stockyard in the state, and they could load up without ever bringing the beef anywhere near Jeopardy.' He turned suddenly to Martha. 'You think that's why Will was killed?'

'Maybe. I don't know. All I can think about now is my boys.' She hunched forward and grabbed him by the arm. 'You were a rancher once, Matt. You could take this place on. I've thought it out. I'll leave you a share, a third of everything we've got here, just so long as you kept the rest for my sons. They'd be working alongside you, learning like they would from Will.'

'Martha—' he began.

'Hear me out. The way I see it, they could buy you out just as soon as they were old enough, if that was what you wanted. Or you could just stay right here. You said you were ready to hang up your gun. This will give you a chance, a different sort of life . . .'

'You think Duke Coulter's going to let that happen?' he said softly.

'If you sold him the south pasture maybe that would be enough.'

'That's the best bit of land you've got. The way Coulter's tightening his stranglehold on Jeopardy he'd never leave me out here anyway. The day would come when I'd meet with an accident, just like Will. It's no good, Martha, it won't work. I figure to get you and your boys away from here, tomorrow.'

'Are you saying we have to abandon this place? Just let Coulter take it?'

'No, but you and your sons shouldn't be here for a while. God willing, I'll settle with Coulter someday, but until then you'd be better off out of harm's way.' He sighed. 'If Monty and Jed don't go chasing off looking to pick a fight with Logan, they could stay and take care of your stock.'

'If you don't tell them what Will said, there's no reason for them to suspect anything.'

'Jed's planning to go up on the bluff, and I don't think there's a thing I can do to stop him. It's been four days; the wind might have blown away some of the signs, but he's real smart when it comes to reading a trail. He'll figure it out. And if he don't, he'll guess something's wrong when we drive out of here tomorrow with the boys.'

Matt watched in silence as Monty finished the last job he'd ever do for Will Trent. At last the cowboy climbed out of the hole he'd dug. 'Can you help me bring him out?'

With a nod Matt followed him to the house, taking the weight of the dead man's feet across his left forearm since he still couldn't use his right hand too well. As they carried the rancher to his grave neither man mentioned Jed's absence, though it lay between them like a shadow.

Martha Trent brought her sons out to stand by the grave. She handed Matt a Bible. 'Be obliged if you'd read over him,' she said, 'I marked the place.'

As Matt opened the book a distant sound made them all look up. Jed Whittaker was coming down the trail, riding like fury. He flung himself off his horse and threw the reins over a fence post. 'Sorry, Mrs Trent.' He snatched off his hat and stood head down beside Monty, breathing hard.

'You—' Monty began.

'Later,' Matt growled. Clearing his throat he read the passage the woman had marked, stumbling over the unfamiliar words. When he'd finished he closed the book and handed it back to her. She turned away, silent tears running down her cheeks, an arm around each of her sons. Roy's face was pale and set, while the younger boy

A PLACE CALLED JEOPARDY

was openly weeping.

The cowboys shovelled dirt into the grave then brought rocks to pile over the dusty earth. At last Monty straightened and looked across the finished mound at his friend. 'Well?'

'Four riders,' Jed replied. 'Chased him flat out from the south pasture. Found a few shells. Seein' he wasn't hit I figure they got the horse.'

Monty looked at Matt. 'You still say he didn't tell you nothing?'

Matt was silent.

'You lied,' Monty said flatly, seeing the truth in Matt's face.

'Yes. It was Logan. Reckoned if I told you the truth you'd stampede into town and get yourselves killed.'

'Guess you don't figure us much,' Monty grated. 'You so sure we'll get beat?'

'Coulter's got five hired guns, maybe more. Harve Rawlins is back in Jeopardy; no reason to think he won't have signed on with Logan, too. I wouldn't bet a nickel on the best two lawmen in the country against odds like that. Besides, no matter how crooked he is, Logan's wearing a badge, and if you plan to ride in and shoot him you'll be putting yourselves outside the law.' Matt grabbed the cowboy by the shoulder. 'See sense, kid. Don't be in such a hurry to die.'

'You think it's better to let Logan get away with murder.' Monty's eyes were alight, his voice shaking with anger. 'That's how Coulter works, keeping folks running scared. Maybe you're talking sense, but I sure as hell can't sit around and do nothing.' He freed himself from Matt's grasp, turned on his heel and disappeared into the barn.

'Can't you stop him?' Matt said, rounding on Jed.

'He's right. This was cold-blooded murder. Folks in Jeopardy need to know the kind of man they've got for a sheriff.'

'You think they don't?' Matt strode alongside Jed as he fetched his horse and went after Monty. 'If it was just Logan and Coulter, I'd ride alongside you boys right now, but there's no point throwing your lives away.'

A small dark-haired figure came dashing from inside the barn and flung itself at Matt, fists flailing. 'You're yellow! I heard what you said. You don't care what they did to Pa—'

'That ain't right, Roy,' Jed said, pinioning the boy's arms and pulling him away. 'The sheriff's hurt. He can't go up against Logan while he can't even tote a gun.'

'He's got two hands, don't he?'

'Don't worry, kid,' Monty said, leading out his horse, 'somebody's going to pay for your pa's death, we'll see to it.'

'Dammit! You think I don't want that too?' Matt raged. 'But take time to think; at least come up with some plan to give yourselves half a chance.'

'We ain't stupid,' Jed said, as the two cowboys mounted. 'No reason for Logan to know we're after him till we make our play.' The two riders swung away, spurring their horses.

For a moment Matt stared after them, then he turned to the boy by his side. 'Help me saddle my horse,' he said resignedly, 'then fetch me your pa's shotgun.'

'Don't go,' Martha begged. She tried to grab the shotgun which Roy was holding, but Matt reached out and took it, dropping it into the holster on his saddle. The woman gripped his arm instead, her fingers digging into his flesh

83

as if she could physically keep him from leaving.

'You said you'd help me. You said you'd see the boys were taken care of—'

'Don't worry, Ma,' the boy said. His eyes were over-bright, his cheeks flushed. 'The sheriff's just going to help Monty and Jed. They're gonna fix Logan, you'll see.' He delved in his pocket to bring out a handful of cartridges which he gave to Matt. 'It's already loaded, but I thought you might need these.'

'Thanks.' Matt eased his arm away from the woman's grasp. 'Don't worry. I'll be right back. Get the wagon hitched, and pack some clothes for you and the boys. You'll need blankets too, and enough food for a week. Roy, help your mother get ready, we'll be leaving soon as I get back from town.'

As he rode away, Matt thought he heard a faint cry. Looking back he saw that Martha was on her knees, her arms around her son. Cursing the two cowboys ahead of him, Matt turned his attention to the trail, trying to come up with some kind of plan that might keep all of them alive.

He rode fast. There was white foam on the animal's neck and flanks by the time Jeopardy came into sight, but he saw nothing of the two riders who'd gone ahead of him. Slowing down he turned off the road, taking a side trail that would bring him into town unseen, the way Rawlins and his companion had ridden a week back. Easing from the saddle he walked the last few yards under the cover of the scrub that spread up from the river.

A horse neighed as Matt peered through the under-brush, and he grasped the bay's nose before it could reply. The cowboys had left their horses tethered to a bush; at least they'd had some sense. Matt left the bay nearby and

84

trod softly across the open space to the back of Kurt Jensen's place, the shotgun cradled in his right arm.

'Kurt?'

The blacksmith stood in the open doorway looking out on to the street. The town was strangely quiet, almost deserted.

Kurt jumped at the sound of Matt's voice. He whipped around. 'Are you crazy? What are you doing back here?'

'Looking for Monty and Jed,' Matt replied. 'They can't have been more than a few minutes ahead of me. You seen them?'

Kurt shook his head. 'Can't say I have. But something's going on. A couple of dozen men came out of the Blue Diamond a while back. It's like they all went to ground; place is so damn quiet now it's like a Sunday. Reckon there's only Coulter's men in there, I haven't seen anything of Logan and his sidekicks.' He paused, cocking his head to one side. 'What's that noise?'

Matt came to stand beside him. The sound was an inter-mittent thudding, like the distant pounding of feet, but there was something else in back of it, a low animal growl. Turning swiftly on his heel, Matt grabbed a shovel and thrust it deep into the forge's fire, bringing out a heap of red hot embers.

'What the . . .' Matt didn't hear the rest of Kurt's protest; he was already sprinting across to the back of the saloon, the shovel held out in front of him. He tipped its contents against the bottom of the wall beneath the room where Mirabelle had died.

'Hey!' It was Sally, sashaying towards him in a grubby robe. Seeing the fire beginning to take hold, the tinder-dry wood disintegrating with a faint crackling sound as the flames licked their way upwards, she took a hurried step towards the door, but Matt grabbed her by the arm, pulling her back.

'Not yet,' he hissed. 'Give it time.'

'But—'

'Reckon there's a couple of friends of mine in there,' Matt went on, jerking his head towards the bar. 'They came to see Logan.'

'You're loco.' Sally spat the words at him, trying to unfasten his grip from her arm. 'Just like them. Whatever they get they asked for it.'

'Like Mirabelle? Did she ask for it, Sally? You know as well as I do that Logan killed her, not Billy.'

'It ain't so! The kid was crazy that day, you saw him.' She sounded like she was pleading with him, and he knew it was herself she was trying to convince. 'He went after Logan with the knife.'

'You don't believe that. Logan's left handed. Admit it, Sally, you saw where those wounds were on Mirabelle's body. It was Billy who went in there and found her dead. It was Billy who took her in his arms as she lay dying, and got covered in her blood. That boy never hurt a living soul.'

She seemed to shrink beneath his hand. 'Duke swore it wasn't Logan,' she whispered.

'You got any good reason for taking the word of a man like Coulter?' Matt asked bleakly.

Sally stared at him wordlessly for a few seconds. 'A girl's gotta live,' she said at last. 'He helped me out when I was down on my luck. Duke was the only one offered me a place when them self-righteous hypocrites turned me out of Serena.'

The wall in front of them was ablaze, the flames leaping to the roof. It was getting uncomfortably hot where they were standing. Sally tried again to pull free. 'What the hell do you think you're doing?'

'Giving myself the edge,' he replied. He pushed her in front of him, in through the doorway which would pretty soon be engulfed by the fire. Small curls of smoke billowed behind them. Matt halted her at a closed door which he knew led into the bar, hearing the sounds from within, knowing with a sick certainty what was happening on the other side.

Matt flung the door open and thrust Sally through it so she fell to her hands and knees. The fire came tearing into the room behind them with a great whoosh, like a huge indrawn breath. Abandoning his hold on the woman, Matt dropped low, diving sideways to take refuge behind the bar. There was nobody there, and he skittered the whole length of the room, praying that Logan's men had been too busy to notice him.

Matt needn't have worried. For a moment the fire, crackling merrily as it devoured floorboards and furniture, wasn't enough to distract the sheriff and his henchmen from their gruesome fun. Eight men were crowding around Monty, who was staggering drunkenly, his head turning bemusedly from side to side as he tried to focus on the giant of a man bearing down on him. It was O'Malley. This time the big man was winning, probably because this was nothing like a fair fight.

'Fire!' Sally regained her feet and ran screaming between chairs and tables to stumble out of the swing doors on to the street. The flames were roaring up the walls now, spreading to the ceiling. In the few seconds before the combat stopped, Matt saw Harve Rawlins kick one of Monty's legs out from under him.

Then Logan and his men were rushing for the door,

pushing to be first out as flakes of hot ash rained down on them. Matt too was running, heading to where Monty, on hands and knees now, was crawling across the floor towards him. That was when Matt saw the thing that lay between them, a crumpled heap of abandoned flesh and blood that had once been a man.

CHAPTER NINE

Jed Whittaker's face had been beaten to a pulp. His mouth and nostrils were filled with blood, congealed and darkening. No bubble of breath escaped from them. Two slit eyes stared sightlessly back at Matt, barely visible among the bruised and swollen flesh. When Matt touched him the man's head lolled grotesquely; his neck was broken.

Swallowing hard, Matt turned his attention to Monty, still on hands and knees and crawling desperately towards Jed's body. Matt raised his voice to sound over the roar of the fire. 'We have to get out of here, Monty. Now.'

The cowboy seemed not to hear. There was an unfocused look about his eyes, and he kept shaking his head as if he was trying to clear it. Despite his obvious confusion, he was still heading unerringly towards his dead friend.

'Monty? Come on, kid.' A crash from above told Matt he was running out of time; the roof was falling in as the flames burnt through the rafters. Monty let out a low moan, more animal than human. Stretching out a hand to Jed the cowboy finally collapsed, his head coming to rest on the dead man's arm. A wisp of smoke rose from the middle of his back where a burning ember had landed.

Matt brushed off the smouldering ash, crouched down

and heaved the young cowboy on to his shoulders, sweat starting on his brow as he forced his injured hand to close around the man's wrist. The door he had pushed Sally through so short a time ago was surrounded by fire, but it was their only means of escape. Through the smoke and heat-haze he could see into the street where men were running to fetch water. He could hear Coulter shouting directions; it would be suicide to go that way.

For a full second Matt hesitated. The heat of the fire was like a solid wall barring his way. Taking a breath, resisting the need to cough as the hot smoky air caught at his throat, he put his head down and ran. One false step and they would both be dead, crisped to a cinder like the charred wood that was raining down in red-hot shards from above. Somehow he kept his feet and burst out into the back yard, sobbing with the effort.

Matt was hardly aware of Kurt Jensen helping to lower Monty from his back, nor did he feel the man's hands beating out the small fires that had started in his clothes. Doubled over, he heaved in fresh air, grunting with the pain of lungs seared by heat and smoke.

'Come on, Matt, we have to get you both out of here before they realized that fire was no accident,' Jensen urged. He bent to lift Monty's apparently lifeless body.

Back under the cover of the trees they manhandled Monty on to the bay, with Matt climbing up behind. Kurt Jensen tied the reins of the other two horses to Matt's saddle.

'Stay out of sight,' Jensen advised, giving the bay a slap of encouragement on the rump. 'Try not to leave any tracks they can follow. Coulter will be howling for blood.'

Matt took the blacksmith's advice, not turning towards the Trent place until he was well out of sight of Jeopardy, then riding up-river through the shallow water for nearly two miles. He pushed the bay as hard as he dared with a double load, twisting constantly in the saddle to look back for any pursuit.

Out on open prairie with the river behind him, Matt stopped to change horses by a heap of boulders, cursing as he struggled to lift Monty's unconscious body from one saddle to the other. The cowboy's face was bleeding and, by the time they moved on, both of them were covered in blood.

At the Circle T, the Trents' wagon stood outside the ranch house, the horses patient between the shafts, a heap of belongings piled haphazardly in the back. There was nobody in sight as Matt pulled Monty from the saddle to place him on top of the load. The cowboy was still unconscious, though when Matt held a canteen to his lips he swallowed some water, and his pulse was beating strong and steady.

Roy Trent appeared as Matt turned Jed's horse out in the corral. The boy's face was pale, his eyes bright as if he had a fever, and his hands were trembling. 'Did you kill Logan?' he asked.

Matt shook his head. 'No. Where's your ma?'

'Out here.' Roy led the way around to the back of the house.

Wielding a shovel too large for him, Ricky stood in a shallow trench beside the heap of fresh-dug dirt that marked his father's grave, tears streaking his filthy face.

'She fell down,' the little boy said.

'She made me bring her writing box.' Roy took a sheet of paper from inside his shirt and handing it to Matt. 'And she said I was to tell you the deeds are in the bedroom, in the drawer.'

Wordlessly Matt took the paper and put it in his pocket. Martha Trent lay by the back door, her Sunday dress half over her head.

'She went to sleep,' Ricky said, 'then she wouldn't wake up.'

'She's dead,' his older brother said harshly, his face screwed up tight, the faintest tremor in his voice as he turned back to Matt, a child trying his best to be a man. 'I knew what we had to do, I saw what she did for Pa, but I couldn't get her clothes on.'

'I'll see to it,' Matt said gently. 'And this,' he added, taking the shovel from Ricky's hands.

'You know where to go?' Matt looked up at the boy who sat holding the reins; at least Will Trent's team were docile, bred for pulling rather than speed.

'Yessir.' The youngster was still dry-eyed, his face pale as candle wax.

'Fine. With luck I'll catch you up tonight, or maybe tomorrow.' He turned to Ricky. 'Your brother's in charge, so you do as you're told, OK? And since he's got enough to think about, I'm relying on you to take care of Monty. Try not to move that shoulder I've strapped up, those bones will take a time to heal, same with his ankle. If he don't come round you have to make sure he has a drink of water every time you do, savvy?'

The youngster nodded. 'And I'll put his blankets over him at night.'

'Good kid. Right, get moving, Roy. And remember, if I don't make it, just keep heading for the Rocking M ranch. Follow that low range of hills like I said. Tell Ches Marryat I sent you.'

Roy Trent's lower lip drooped a fraction, then he

straightened his back and nodded, slapping the reins on the broad rumps of the horses and clicking his tongue at them.

As the youngster drove away, Matt brushed out the wheel ruts with his boot. He loaded Monty's roan with a couple of sacks of feed and a barrel of water; anyone with half Jed's skill at tracking would notice if only one horse was packing a weight, and Matt needed Logan to believe he was following two men, not one.

Once the wagon was out of sight Matt opened the gate of the corral, hazing the horses with his hat to drive them out, and on to the trail that the youngsters had taken. Mounting the bay and leading Monty's cowpony, he followed, careful to obscure any signs of the wagon's passing.

Looking back towards Jeopardy he could see smoke still billowing into the sky above a patch of grey haze; it looked like the fire might have spread some. Coulter wouldn't be too happy watching his town go up in smoke, he owned most of that block alongside the Blue Diamond. The thought brought a grim smile to Matt's face. With luck, Logan and the rest of Coulter's men would be fighting the flames for a while yet. He just hoped Kurt Jensen still had a roof over his head.

Where the trail split, Matt rode on after the wagon for a while, herding the loose horses in front of him. Fifty yards on he stopped and the beasts slowed to a walk, but they were still drifting after the wagon; there was a water-hole a mile ahead, and in the sweltering heat Matt figured they'd keep going until they reached it.

Picking up a piece of brush to rub out the hoof marks left by his two horses, Matt turned aside to rejoin the road that led west towards the mountains. He was careful not to make too good a job of hiding his tracks. He needed Logan to follow him; that way he wouldn't discover the wagon.

As the day ended, Matt was high in the hills. He halted his horse on top of a ridge and looked back. Far below on the prairie he could see a group of riders, close bunched. Five of them he thought, though it was hard to judge as the light faded.

Suddenly the riders picked up their pace, and he realized they must have seen him, silhouetted against the fiery sunset. With luck at this distance the load on Monty's horse would look enough like a man draped over the saddle to fool them. Matt rode on, down off the skyline and into the growing darkness. Unlike the men on his tail, he knew this country. Logan wouldn't catch him here.

For the whole of the next day Matt kept moving on through the hills, waiting for Logan to quit trailing him. Trouble was, Jeopardy's new sheriff wasn't giving up and, with each passing hour, he'd moved inexorably closer. Until now. Just when Matt was beginning to think he'd have to ride all the way to the west coast to lose him, Logan vanished.

Although it was what he'd wanted, the prickle at the back of Matt's neck told him this wasn't good news. In the jumble of rocky gullies and steep ridges it was too easy for men to hide, and he recalled how close he'd come to catching Harve Rawlins.

One man alone was easy meat. Only the belief that Monty was riding alongside the one-time sheriff had kept Logan's men at a distance so far. With five men on his tail, Matt was uneasily aware that if just one of them got close enough to realize their mistake, he was finished, and he was beginning to suspect Logan had somebody with him who knew the territory.

Matt pressed the bay harder, increasing his speed. The roll of the dice was no longer going his way. As he headed down a dry gully, taking the slope a little too fast for safety, the bay suddenly lost its footing and slid back on its haunches. Matt stayed in the saddle, but as his body swayed backwards he heard the crack of a shot. A slug zipped past his head, missing him by a whisker. They'd found him.

Matt let go of Monty's roan, which went plunging on down the steep gulch. Assuming the bullet had come from below he dragged the bay's head around and drove it uphill, crouching low over the saddlebow. He looked back over his shoulder, scanning the rocks that lined the gully on either side, trying to locate the man who'd fired at him, all the time urging the bay faster. It was a bad decision. Turning back to face the way he was going, he blinked as sunlight flashed blindingly off a gun barrel. Uphill and straight ahead of him.

As Matt whipped round again another shot cracked past. The roan had hightailed it so fast, it was already dropping out of sight, but with Matt beating his heels against its ribs the bay was more than willing to try and catch it up. The bay careered recklessly down the steep gully. Every step was perilous. A river of loose stone had been set in motion by the horses' hoofs, and Matt grasped the saddle horn as his mount crashed back on its haunches again. This time it didn't recover, falling sideways when it could find no purchase for its front feet. Matt kicked free, just getting his leg out of the way before it got caught between the saddle and the torrent of rock beneath.

For a split second the horse was still with him, and Matt

pulled Will Trent's shotgun from its holster, then the beast fell away, picking up speed as it plummeted helplessly down the gully. Matt rolled, escaping from the torrent of tumbling stone and coming to rest against the side of the gulch where he was in the lee of a boulder. It wasn't much, but he had some cover and with luck he might stay alive.

The man who had shot at him came running down the gully. It was Mendez. He had a rifle in his hands, and having shortened the range he slowed to snap off a shot, which zinged over Matt's head. Matt wriggled back another yard, robbing the man of his target.

'Hold it, Mendez, stop right there.' The shotgun to his shoulder, Matt sighted along the barrel. 'Throw down the gun.'

Mendez was close enough for Matt to see his face, the look of contempt giving way to alarm as he realized his predicament.

'Last chance,' Matt said, lifting a little so Mendez could see he had the drop on him. 'Throw down the gun or you're a dead man.'

'Ain't me headin' for boot hill,' Mendez sneered, sliding to a halt and lifting the rifle to his shoulder. 'So long, old man.'

Matt ducked back, feeling the hot breath of Mendez's shot as it skimmed past his cheek. He fired, glad to find his injured hand wasn't too painful as he squeezed the trigger, though the kick of the scattergun sent him sliding further downhill.

Mendez fell on his face, the rifle dropping away from him, and slithered helplessly down the slope. He came to rest against the boulder where Matt had taken shelter. Matt stood up and looked down into eyes filled with a mix of pain and fury; Mendez's chest was a mangled mess; he didn't have long to live.

'Damn you! That five hundred bucks was as good as mine,' Mendez ground out. Blood bubbled up into his mouth. He choked, and died.

Matt picked up the dead man's rifle and turned to go after the horses, half running, half sliding, as the rocks shifted under his feet. He skidded to a precarious halt where the ground dropped away suddenly. There was a ten foot sheer drop before him. When the rains came this would be a racing cataract, but now the channel was dry, and the bowl down below him held only a few inches of water. The two horses must have made the jump, unless they fell. They were milling restlessly together in the pool, unsettled and sweating but apparently having come to no harm.

Finding footholds in the cliff, Matt let himself down over the drop, stopping to gentle the horses for a moment then going past them to peer down beyond the lip of the shallow bowl. There was another sheer drop, but only about three foot. After that the gully widened and the slope grew less. He had a way out.

Sounds echoed from above and behind him. Another man was coming down the gulch. Matt was about to make a dash for his horse when he saw movement on the hillside off to his left. Two birds rose rapidly into the sky, making shrill cries of protest at being disturbed, while from somewhere below he heard a horse neighing. He was wrong about the way out. Logan's men had him surrounded.

Taking another look at the way the water had carved out the hillside, Matt led his horse to stand below the dry waterfall. He reloaded the scattergun, then broke open the rifle. Four shots.

Climbing up to stand on the bay's saddle, Matt found a

foothold so he could hoist his shoulders over the top of the sheer rock face. The bearded man, Zeke, had stopped beside Mendez's body. A single shot was enough to discourage him, and he backed off, scrabbling wildly at the loose rocks with his hands as they threatened to send him sliding into Matt's sights.

Matt dropped back into the hollow and ran across to the other side. A couple more shots brought stillness to the hillside below, and he hunkered down, thinking hard. He was secure in his hideout, but Logan had him locked up tight.

The day was nearing its end. By now Logan must know Matt was alone. There was a good chance the sheriff's men would close in under cover of darkness. Which meant he had a couple of hours to come up with some way out of the mess he was in.

'Easy now,' Matt whispered, running a hand down the bay's neck. 'Stand right there. Everything's fine.'

The horse stood on the lip of the shallow bowl, the drop beneath its feet unseen in the darkness that shrouded the mountains. Behind the bay the roan shifted uneasily. Matt chewed on his lip. The plan wasn't perfect, but it was the best he could come up with. He let himself silently over the drop, putting his feet down carefully on the loose rocks at the bottom, relieved when the horses made no attempt to follow.

Several minutes later Matt was on level ground. He caught the scent of horses and heard the faint creak of leather; Logan had kept his horses saddled. Though Matt couldn't see where the animals were tethered he knew it had to be close.

Lowering himself to the ground, Matt slithered on his

belly, his Colt in his hand and his heart pounding.

If his guess was wrong and Logan had drawn all his men in for the night, then the next few minutes could be his last.

CHAPTER TEN

Matt Turner lay under a pile of brush, hardly daring to breathe. He was so close to the man keeping watch over Logan's horses that he could smell him, a reeking mix of unwashed flesh and stale whiskey. For some reason the stink seemed familiar. The darkness was total down here below the steep hillside and Matt could see nothing. He didn't want to make any further move until the moon rose; there was just a chance that more than one man awaited him, and the odds were already stacked uncomfortably in Logan's favour.

Time dragged so slow Matt felt like it had stopped; his weary brain wondered crazily if it was possible to die without noticing. Maybe he'd lie here in the dark for ever. A couple of yards away one of the horses moved restlessly, stamping a hoof.

'Quiet down,' the sentinel hushed. There was a light chink of glass as a bottle knocked against something, then the man began to sing, the words slightly slurred and so soft they were barely audible. 'That old Buckskin he threw me, and tromped on my head . . .'

Matt couldn't believe what he was hearing. He knew that voice. No wonder he'd recognized the smell. He'd listened to that song a hundred times, when Two Shots rolled home with a skinful. If the old reprobate couldn't find the door of his ramshackle lean-to he'd lie curled up under the sidewalk outside the sheriff's office, and serenade him from there. On winter nights Matt heaved him inside, afraid that otherwise he'd find him dead from cold the next morning.

Bitter thoughts drew hard lines on Matt's face. It looked like the old man had sold out, offering him into the hands of Logan's hired killers in exchange for a couple of bottles of whiskey.

Matt wanted to be a few miles away by dawn, but still he waited. Two choruses later nobody had told the old man to shut up, so it looked as if he was alone. The way his voice slurred over the words it sounded like Two Shots had been drinking quite a while; any other man would be about ready for sleep, but it took a lot of booze to knock out the old drunkard. Trouble was, Two Shots might not be thinking too straight by now, and start yelling before Matt had a chance to silence him.

Carefully Matt rose to his knees, resisting the temptation to groan as cramp seized him. A shape became visible, leaning against a rock, and just a little more solid than the blackness surrounding him. There was the sound of liquid sloshing as the bottle was lifted yet again.

As soon as his blood was circulating and he was sure he could stand upright, Matt got to his feet. Moving fast, he slammed the end of the Colt's barrel into the old man's ribs, bringing his right forearm against the scrawny neck. 'Not a squeak,' he hissed, 'or so help me I'll give you what you deserve, you two-timing old soak.'

Despite the warning, Two Shots gave a petrified squawk, though it was choked off before it got past his teeth. He

101

twitched under Matt's hand, then the sound of running water hitting the ground brought a new odour with it, and Matt felt a warm wetness trickling down inside his boot. 'Dammit!' he breathed, jerking back.

The old man was shaking. 'Matt?' he whispered. 'What you wanna jump me like that for?'

'Shh, keep your voice down. You've done me enough good turns, bringing Logan down on me.'

'I didn't know it was you we was followin'.' Two Shots protested.

'Give me one good reason to believe you.' Matt lifted the old man off his feet and shook him.

'Hell, you know me. I ain't no back shooter. Wasn't till this mornin' I figured maybe somethin' was wrong, when I got close enough to take a look at that bay of yours.'

'So then you helped Logan get me boxed up in that gully,' Matt said angrily. 'Sure sounds like you're trying to sell me a heap of horse-shit.'

'That's not how it was. I asked Logan about the bay. He told me that sidewinder Rawlins must be ridin' your horse. He had some story about you lettin' Rawlins out of jail in the first place. Matt, it wasn't my fault. He bought me a couple of bottles, an' before I knowed it, he got me so mixed up I didn't know what to think.'

'Seems you did enough thinking to decide to give Logan a hand. You drunken old coot, how much is he paying you?'

'He was gonna turn me out,' Two Shots whined. 'That place of mine ain't much, but I gotta have a roof over my head. Trust me, Matt, I wouldn't be here if I'd knowed it was you. It coulda been Rawlins. He was in town, that night the boys sneaked you out to Trent's place.'

'I know, I saw him. In fact I figured he might be out

here right now, giving Logan a hand.'

'A man with the federal marshals after him, ridin' with a posse? Even Logan wouldn't risk that.'

'A posse?' Matt hissed. 'You saying this bunch of gunslingers call themselves a posse?'

'Logan swore 'em in, I was there. When word got around about Jed Whittaker gettin' killed a whole lot of townsfolk turned up and wanted to know what Logan planned to do about it. Some of 'em wanted to ride with us but he turned 'em down. Said they wasn't needed, but that him an' the posse would bring in the murderer.'

'What?' Matt let the old man go, a sick feeling in his belly. '*They* killed Jed. Beat the poor kid to a pulp then broke his neck.'

'Logan said he died in the fire, an' that he'd find the man who started it. He made a big play of gettin' justice for the kid 'cos he'd been left to burn to death in the saloon. The way he told it, Jed was knocked out cold when he tried to stop somebody settin' light to the Blue Diamond.'

'And people believed him?'

Two Shots shrugged. 'Nobody wasn't arguin'. Logan could've had three times as many men, but apart from me he only brought Coulter's gunslingers. They ain't too good at reading signs, guess that's why they wanted me along.' Two Shots glanced uneasily around. 'Look, Matt, you can't blame me for helpin' Logan tail you, not when you was actin' like some greenhorn. I never saw such an easy trail to read, you coulda lost us a dozen times if you'd been tryin'.'

'I didn't want to lose him. But I didn't plan on letting him get men ahead of me to pin me down that way. You sure made a good job of it.'

'I'm real sorry, Matt. I figured Rawlins was a pretty dumb-cluck leavin' tracks half wiped an' all. Never crossed my mind we was followin' you. I thought you was safe out at Will's place.'

'With Will Trent dead and Duke Coulter trying to move in on his land? I'm safer out here.'

'Yeah, well, maybe you're right. What're you gonna do now?'

'I'm heading east. I'll need to find somebody to swear a warrant against the men who really killed Whittaker, and I figure Marshal Brand will help me. He won't pay no mind to Logan's stories.'

'You figure to ride all the way to Kansas?'

'Heck, no. There's plenty of places I can jump a train.'

Two Shots looked unconvinced. 'You better be careful. That man Roper's up and down the line pretty much all the time, an' you don't wanna meet that tame grizzly o' his.'

'I'll keep out of their way. Just so long as you keep Logan off my heels. When I ride out of here I'll lay a false trail, head south a mile or two.' Suddenly Matt realized he could see the outline of the five horses. The moon had risen.

'I've got to get moving. Logan's going to know I was here, so I'd better make this look good.' He drew back his left fist, then paused. 'You let them think I knocked you cold. And when you come after me next time, you make damn sure you get this so-called posse lost.'

Two Shots nodded, screwing his eyes tight shut as Matt swung at his chin. Pulling the punch just before it hit, Matt was a little concerned when the blow knocked the old man clean off his feet. He leant down anxiously, peering at the blood welling from the drunkard's lip. 'OK?'

'I'll live,' Two Shots mumbled. 'Don't you worry none about me, I'll take care of Logan. Go on, get out o' here.'

Matt went to the horse line and quietly untied the animals. They stayed where they were, only one shifting a little as he released it. Hurrying back to the bottom of the ravine he'd climbed down hours before, Matt looked up. The bay wasn't visible, the gully still shrouded in shadow.

For a second Matt hesitated, measuring the risks; he could steal a couple of horses and get away without creating a ruckus, but that would put him on the wrong side of the law. The time might come when he'd step across that invisible line, but this wasn't it.

Putting his fingers to his mouth Matt whistled, the shrill sound cutting through the silence. A man shouted from somewhere high above, but there was no response from the gully. Matt whistled again, and this time he saw a dim shape moving up above as his horse jumped down over the lip of the dry waterfall.

Suddenly it was all noise. Gunfire crashed through the night. The five horses belonging to the posse leapt back in alarm and discovered they were free. For the moment they stayed together, a spinning snorting bunch of muscled horseflesh milling uneasily in the near darkness. The bay was invisible in the shadows, but the clatter of metal-shod hoofs on rock told Matt the horse was careering down the steep slope in answer to his call.

Matt focused on the sound, seeing the fast approaching shape as it plunged out of the gully. Suddenly the bay was right beside him and he leapt, grabbing a handful of mane. He swung himself up and landed in the saddle, taking hold of the rein he'd looped loosely around the pommel.

Another salvo echoed in the hills, but the men were

firing wildly in the dark and, as far as he could tell, none of their shots came near. The posse's horses scattered as Matt and the bay went powering through them. Matt grinned to himself. A bullet zinged by and he flinched, but he was safe enough; in the confusion Logan's men would likely find themselves shooting their own horses.

'Hold your fire,' Logan shouted, as if he'd read Matt's thought. The crack of a solitary shot echoed off the rock face, then there was only the sound of hoofs to disturb the night. 'Turner! I'll get you! I'll hunt you down. Ain't nowhere you can hide!'

The bay was flat out, heading across open prairie. Hearing hoofbeats close on his tail, Matt looked back, his heart pounding. Monty's roan was right behind them, neck stretched as it raced to keep up. Matt let out a whoop of triumph and eased his horse's head towards the south. A couple of miles away there was a dry river-bed, the ideal place to lay his false trail.

Noon found Matt high in the hills, approaching a rocky peak known as Look-out Point. Leaving the horses in a sheltered arroyo where a little grass grew among the damp stones, he climbed to the summit, careful not to show himself on the skyline. Settling himself comfortably against the rock Matt tipped his hat to shade his eyes and scanned the prairie spread out below. If Two Shots had done his job properly the posse would still be trying to follow his false trail.

All the wide prospect lying below him to the south was empty of life. He turned to look eastwards. There, far off, a haze of dust rose. Matt squinted at the tiny black shapes below the dust cloud, making out men and horses heading away from him, moving fast. Far too fast to be following a trail, and anyway they were nowhere near the track he'd laid with such care during the night.

Abruptly Matt jerked to his feet; there were only three men. Of the five horses, one of those without a rider shone pale in the sun. Two Shots had been riding a grey.

Matt made fast time, trusting the bay to keep its feet as they hurtled downhill, no longer concerned to hide his passing but taking the shortest route back to the place where he'd left the old man. Some instinct of self-preservation made him swing wide, so he rode back to the old campsite along the tracks of the riders heading east, now long since out of sight. He tucked himself snugly below the steeply rising cliff. Logan might be a thug, but he was a thug with a brain; it was just possible this was a trap. Almost hoping that was true, Matt pulled up in a flurry of dust and stepped down from the saddle, taking the shotgun from its holster.

Two Shots wasn't by the boulders where Matt had knocked him down the night before. There was nobody by the ashes of the fire, nor where the scuffed earth and drying heaps of droppings marked the horse line. Matt walked cautiously to the bottom of the gully, the shotgun in his hand. Crows flew up as he approached, croaking their protest, and a coyote, half seen in the shadows, slunk off up the ravine and disappeared.

A dark shape dangled in mid-air, suspended above the tumble of stone. Choking back a curse, Matt ran, scrabbling over the rocks. Two Shots hung by his wrists, his body swaying gently. The men who left him there had secured a line to each side of the ravine, then heaved the old man up until the rope was stretched taut.

It wasn't an easy climb, but in a couple of minutes Matt had the rope in his hand. It looked as if the old man was dead, but Matt couldn't be sure and he feared to let his old friend slam against the opposite wall of the ravine. He fought to release the knot, and once it was free he let out half the line then tied it again. Throwing himself down recklessly and across the gully, he clambered up to do the same thing the other side.

Two Shots hung only a couple of feet from the ground. Sobbing for breath Matt regained the bottom of the gully and leapt to slash through the rope. He caught the old man's body as it fell, feeling the bones through their thin covering of flesh.

His care had been for nothing; the body was cold. The eyes were missing, pecked out by a bird. The scrawny old feet, bare beneath the ragged ends of his pants, were damaged too. But it hadn't been a crow or a coyote that had reduced the living flesh and bone to shapeless lumps of bloody meat: that had been the work of a two-legged animal.

Mirabelle and Billy, Will Trent, Jed Whittaker and now Two Shots.

'Logan.' Matt breathed. Then he filled his lungs, threw back his head and yelled in helpless fury. '*Logan!*' The word echoed around the hills and came back to him in a hundred voices. 'I swear,' Matt said quietly, 'I'll make that man pay, if it takes every last day of my life.'

CHAPTER ELEVEN

Matt shook up the reins and the two horses lumbered into a trot. He glanced at Roy Trent, riding alongside on Monty's roan. The boy urged the cowpony to a jog, his feet almost bouncing out of the irons as the horse kicked up its heels. Roy had barely spoken to Matt since he'd caught up with the wagon the day before, but the kid had gotten up on the roan that morning, and Matt hadn't argued, word-lessly helping to shorten the leathers.

'You want to ride the bay?' he asked suddenly, turning to the back of the wagon, where the younger boy sat at Monty's side. Ricky Trent shook his head.

'Could be Monty might need some water,' he said. His hand was clutched tightly on the cowboy's shirt sleeve, his knuckles white. Matt sighed. The kid had just lost his father and his mother, and left the only home he'd ever known. It wasn't surprising he hung on so tight to this man, his one connection to a childhood being torn apart with such brutal finality. Every hour was taking him and his brother further from the Circle T and into the unknown.

It was likely the boy was in for another hard knock; Monty was showing no sign of regaining consciousness. A man could live a few weeks without food, but he couldn't go on that way forever. Matt was beginning to wonder if the cowboy would simply drift into death without ever coming round.

The wagon topped a rise and there before them was a cluster of buildings, no more than half a mile away. Almost as if they scented the end of the journey the team picked up their pace.

'Is that where your friend lives?' Ricky asked.

'That's it.' Matt was suddenly very tired. He felt at least twice his forty-four years, and he recalled he'd hardly slept in a week.

The Rocking M ranch lay quiet and deserted, the grey of its timber walls turned pink by the light of the evening sun. Matt brought the team to a halt in the yard. Ricky climbed over from his place beside Monty to sit on the seat with him. 'He'll get better here, won't he?' he asked anxiously, looking back over his shoulder at the injured cowboy.

'Sure he will,' Matt said, hoping it wasn't a lie. 'He was better off being out cold, what with all that jolting around in the wagon. Ain't easy for the body to mend when it gets no rest.' Turning, he checked that Roy was behind them. The boy pulled up, holding back as if to distance himself from the wagon and the man driving it. Matt had tried talking to the kid, but it was like talking to a wall.

'Anybody home?' Matt called, facing the ranch house again and looping the reins around the brake.

The door swung open and a slight figure stood in the shadowed doorway. Matt's mouth dropped open and for a second the world spun, just the way it had when he'd been running a fever. 'Betsy?' he breathed, so soft it was doubtful even the kid at his side heard him.

The girl stepped into the light. She was maybe twenty

years old, with blue-black hair swept back from her fore-head, and a trim figure shown off to perfection in a plain cotton dress. Her gaze rested on Matt's stubbly face and dishevelled figure for the briefest moment, then she looked at the two boys, giving them a smile that would have reduced the kids to mush if they'd been a few years older. 'Something we can do for you folks?'

'Looking for Ches Marryat,' Matt said, trying to cover his confusion. He swallowed hard. It had been a long time, but he felt he should have known that Ches had fathered a child, particularly one who looked like this. Now he saw her plain he realized this wasn't Betsy, couldn't be. But apart from the tilt of her nose and being maybe an inch or two taller, she looked just the way Ches Marryat's sister had looked the last time Matt saw her. That had been nigh on twenty-three years ago, a few weeks before she ran off to marry John Badon.

Matt felt a pain somewhere inside, under his breast bone. His lip curled with an old, long-practised cynicism. There was no such thing as a broken heart; he was just lacking a decent meal and a comfortable place to lay his head for a few hours.

'He's gone to fetch some horses, but he'll be back any time. You're welcome to step down and wait.'

'We've an injured man here,' Matt said, going round to the rear of the wagon. 'Got some broken bones. And he's been out cold for a week.'

The girl was instantly beside him, and before he could even offer her a hand she was climbing on to the wagon. Gently she caressed the cowpoke's bruised cheek. 'The poor boy! What happened to him? You'd better help me move him into the bunkhouse, there's more room there, and the stove is alight. We'll need hot water.'

111

'You'll get blood on you,' Matt cautioned. 'That cut on his chin opened up again this morning, it's been slow to heal.'

'Never mind that.' She was already easing her hands under Monty's neck. 'Here, I'll support his head.' They began to ease him from the wagon. 'The poor boy,' she said again.

At that moment the cowboy's eyes opened, then widened in alarm as he stared up at the girl. 'My lord!' He sounded terrified.

'Monty?' Matt had just taken the whole of the cowboy's weight in his arms, but now he paused, afraid the youngster wasn't right in the head. Maybe the beating he'd taken had addled his brain. 'You OK, kid?'

'My lord,' Monty croaked again, his eyes swivelling to look at Matt. 'That you, Sheriff? Sure am glad to see you. For a moment there I thought I'd woke up dead.'

There was the rustle of skirts and a light footstep on the veranda. Matt didn't see her come, but suddenly another figure was beside him, a faint sweet perfume filling his head as she leant in close, to cluck sympathetically over the damage to Monty's face. The cowboy groaned. 'Heck, now there's two of 'em.'

Matt looked at the newcomer and his legs almost buckled. This time there was no mistake. 'Betsy!'

She was quite composed, her expression dispassionate, her voice calm. 'Good evening, Mr Turner. I think we'd better get the young man inside, don't you? Before you drop him.'

'How long have they been here?' Matt asked, keeping his voice pitched low. He and Ches Marryat were sitting on the veranda, smoking companionably, and staring at the great spread of stars above their heads.

'Five years. Ever since John Badon died. Betsy wrote me. Said she thought it would do Laura good to have a spell of peace and quiet. They pitched up here a couple of months later, and somehow they never got around to leaving. Don't reckon Betsy ever took too well to life back East, too many people in them big cities.'

'But she stayed with Badon until he died.'

'Yeah.' Ches blew a smoke ring. 'You know my sister. Always the same. Once she made her mind up to something she stuck by it.'

Matt was silent, thinking. She hadn't stuck by him. A bit of luck with a silver lode had given him and Ches enough money to buy the Rocking M, and Ches's widowed mother had come to keep house, grateful for something useful to do. Naturally she'd brought her daughter along with her. Matt had spent almost a year courting Betsy Marryat.

That summer had been the happiest he'd ever known. He'd start work before dawn so he finished in time to take his girl out riding, once the heat of the day had gone. Most Sundays he'd drive her to Dewsburg to church, taking nearly three hours each way, just the two of them in Mrs Marryat's old buggy. He'd rarely roused her old horse out of a walk. Even now the thought of it brought a smile to his face. By August he and Betsy had been talking about the cabin they'd build, a half-mile from the ranch house, how one day they'd set up in a place of their own.

Maybe he should have seen the warning signs. John Badon had been around, coming to call whenever he was passing. He'd even taken Betsy to a Sunday social when Matt was busy at roundup time, but Matt had been sure of his girl's affections. Betsy had treated the small-town lawyer kindly enough, but then, she was that sort of person. The poorest drifter or hobo would always get a friendly word and a decent meal while Betsy was at the Rocking M.

All through that year she'd given no hint of preferring Badon to Matt as a suitor, though once or twice Matt felt uneasy; the ranch was scraping them a living but his prospects were pretty poor in comparison to a man of the law. Especially one who had powerful friends back East.

Then the winter had set in, a time of bitter winds and driving snow, and suddenly everything changed. Marshal Hartley had ridden out from Dewsburg, looking for men to help him track down a fugitive. The man had killed a storekeeper in the town, then hightailed it into the hills. Although Betsy begged him not to go, Matt had signed on as a deputy. Two months later they brought the wanted man in, though the posse was two men short by that time, and the rest of them were close to starving. Coming back to the Rocking M, nothing but skin and bone, Matt had found Betsy gone. The end of a dream.

Ches Marryat stubbed out his cigarette and flung the butt out into the yard, bringing Matt back to the present.

'I'll be moving on,' Matt said.

'Figured you'd say that.' Ches glanced sidelong at his old friend. 'But you don't have to go. My two cowhands will be here in a few days; they're good men, we'll back you if there's trouble.'

'It'll take more than four of us to take Logan. If he comes he'll bring plenty of company.' He sighed. 'Can't figure what to do for the best.'

'Stay awhile at least, rest up a bit. No reason for Logan to find you here. I'm willing to bet not even a darned Apache could follow your trail once you set your mind to

114

losing him. And with Logan thinking you've headed east . . .'

Clenching his jaw, Matt wondered why he'd told Two Shots that lie. It had never crossed his mind that Logan would torture a helpless old man to death to wring information out of him. What Logan had learned hadn't been totally untrue, in time Matt would go east and seek out Jay Brand. If he could get a couple of federal marshals on his side there might be a chance of shoehorning Duke Coulter and his hired gunslingers out of Jeopardy.

Matt stubbed out his cigarette on the sole of his boot. 'I don't know. Coming to the Rocking M seemed like a good idea, but I didn't know you'd got two women under your roof. And if Logan finds me he'll find the youngsters.'

'One pair of boys look pretty much like another, I'll swear every which way these two are my nephews.' Ches grinned. 'Heck, I got a niece, so why not?'

'It's real good of you to take them in. They've had a pretty bad time. Tell the truth I couldn't think what else to do with them,' Matt admitted.

'Plenty of room, and I reckon they'll make 'emselves useful, once they settle. Besides, it'll give Betsy somebody to fuss over, seeing Laura's put a rope on that cowboy.'

'Gave him quite a shock when he woke up to see her leaning over him,' Matt said. 'He thought he'd died and gone to heaven.'

'A man heals better when he's got a woman to tend his broken bones,' Ches said with mock solemnity. He paused. 'Talking of which, how's that hand feeling?'

'It's fine. Mending real pretty all by itself. And you can quit looking at me that way. You're right, Mrs Badon asked the same thing, and she got the same answer.'

Ches snorted. 'You got a ramrod shoved up your backside? Her name's Betsy.'

Matt didn't reply and silence fell again. The door of the bunkhouse opened, and Laura came out carrying a tray, calling goodnight to her patient. Her face was prettily flushed as she passed the two older men and vanished indoors.

'Might be a kindness not to let them get too fond,' Matt said, his voice suddenly harsh.

Ches looked at him in surprise. 'Why's that? You ain't got notions about a city girl being too good for a cowhand? Laura's been here long enough to know her own mind; she don't hanker for the life back East.'

Matt shook his head. 'Sometime soon Monty's going to remember what Logan did to his best friend. Once he's mended he'll be looking for revenge.'

'And what about you?' Ches asked. 'What are you looking for?'

Matt stared up at the dark sky. 'Peace of mind, maybe,' he replied. 'Guess you'll understand when I say a man gets to feel his age. If I'd had any sense I'd have handed in my badge a couple of years back. But I figured it didn't matter if it took longer to pull my boots on some mornings, or that I ran out of breath a time or two. There was nobody but me to notice I was slowing down.'

'Same for all of us,' Ches said. 'But all them years of experience, reckon I'd back that against some young whippersnapper who's still wet behind the ears. Even if he has got a full set of teeth,' he added mournfully, spitting a shred of tobacco though a gap in his own.

'I beat you there,' Matt replied. 'Haven't lost any of mine yet.' He sighed. 'Too late for wishing. I was too damn comfortable. I hung on to my job, Duke Coulter moved in and before I knew it I was in a mess of trouble. Which

means there's unfinished business back in Jeopardy. A lot
of good folks are going to have a hard time, unless somebody deals with that bastard.'

'No reason why that has to be you.'

'You know better than that, Ches. Like young Monty,
I've got some debts to pay.'

'You don't have to leave.' Betsy had her back to him, her
floury hands pummelling a lump of dough. 'Not on my
account.'

'Thanks, but I figured I'd sit out on the veranda,' Matt
said, pouring coffee from the pot on the stove. He'd been
at the ranch three days, and somehow the two of them had
avoided being alone together until now.

'That wasn't what I meant: I was talking about you leaving the Rocking M. It would make sense to wait until your
hand's properly healed. Ches thinks you should stay.'

He turned and looked at her. She still had the fine
figure she'd had as a girl, and her dark hair showed no
hint of grey. 'Seem to recall another occasion when I was
leaving and you begged me not to go.'

'That was a long time ago.' There was a faint tremor in
her voice as she went on, 'I don't suppose what I want will
make any difference now, any more than it did then.'

'Betsy!' He went around the table, but she kept her
neck bent as if intent on her work, hiding her face from
him. 'I never did understand why it was so all-fired important to you that I didn't ride with that posse.'

'Didn't you?' She lifted her head then, her eyes ablaze.
'Well, that's men for you, blind as bats, every one. I
suppose I have to spell it out.' She put her hands on her
hips, a stance that was instantly familiar to him. 'I knew
you weren't cut out to be a rancher, though the Lord

117

knows you tried, I have to give you that. Poor Matt. I could see it in your face, every time that wretched man asked you to ride on a posse. Something inside had you cut out to be a lawman.'

'But that was the first time,' Matt protested. 'Heck, I turned Marshal Hartley down twice that summer.'

'I know. And you did it for me. I appreciate that. But in the end the need was too great, and off you went. You nearly got yourself killed too.' Betsy went back to her work, thumping even harder.

'How did you know about that?' He was getting angry too, now, and he grabbed her by the shoulders, making her meet his eyes. 'You were gone, run off with Badon, weeks before I came home.'

She pulled free, her own temper flaring in tune with his. A floury hand struck him hard across the face. 'You dumb-cluck! My mother wrote me. I told her to. You think I didn't care? When you left I didn't sleep for a week. I spent every moment worrying. And when I did sleep I had terrible dreams, seeing you shot, or knifed, or frozen to death.' Her tone was suddenly soft, pleading with him to understand. 'I couldn't live that way, Matt. And I knew it was what you wanted. You were born to be a lawman. If I'd forced you to stay here on the ranch you never would have been happy.'

CHAPTER TWELVE

Matt was speechless. For years he'd puzzled over the reason for Betsy's desertion, and he'd never come close to figuring out the truth. 'But . . .' he stammered at last, 'dammit woman, that's crazy. You never gave me a chance! You could've let me try!'

'Yes. I could.' There were unshed tears in Betsy's eyes. 'I was nineteen years old, Matt. Girls of nineteen aren't too good at thinking straight, especially when they're in love.'

She was in his arms then, her head pressed to his vest, her body soft and warm against his, her hands putting smears of flour on his clothes and his face. They were silent a long time, then at last she drew a deep shuddering breath. 'I'm sorry,' she said. 'When you appeared out of nowhere yesterday I tried so hard not to care, not to feel anything.'

'Had me fooled,' he said softly, stroking her hair. 'You were so darned calm.'

'I was watching you through the window, not daring to come out until I'd stopped shaking.'

Pushing away suddenly she looked at him, her head tilting defiantly. 'Don't get me wrong, I hold by what I did. John Badon was a good husband, we had a happy life together. And I was right about you. When you rode back to the Rocking M half starved and near frozen, you had no intention of handing back that badge you were wearing. You weren't cut out to be a rancher, Matt Turner.'

'I'll prove you wrong,' he said, pulling her to him again. 'I swear to God, Betsy, I'm done with the law. Just as soon as this business is settled . . .'

She gave a shaky laugh and he stopped, frowning down at her.

'This is where we started,' he said. 'You were asking me not to go. But if I don't, then those two young boys you're getting so fond of are going to die. Coulter wants the land they inherited from their father, and he won't let a couple of children stand in his way. It may take time, but one day Logan will track them down.'

'You've got me wrong again, Matt,' she said. 'I know you have to finish this thing. Apart from anything else, I have no intention of marrying you while you're on the run from the law!'

Matt was lost. 'But weren't you saying I shouldn't leave?'

'Yes, but you weren't listening, as usual. I said, not until your hand is healed. I heard you talking to Ches, I know you can use a shotgun, though it doesn't come easy. But that's not going to be enough, is it?' She stood on tiptoe and kissed him. 'Wait. Please.'

'You don't have to worry.' He put her gently away from him. 'I'm not that much of a fool, When I ride away from here I won't be going anywhere near Coulter, or that snake Logan. But I guess you're right, a few days won't hurt. Meantime, you can cosset me all you want. And did I get you right? Did I hear you say something about us getting married? Seems to me a man's supposed to be the one to bring that up.'

'You did,' she replied, her cheeks dimpling. 'Twenty-three years ago.'

'I walked all the way to the corral and back,' Monty said, stepping away from the corner of the bunkhouse into the yard, as if to prove he didn't need its support. The warm wind howling around the buildings whipped up the dust and tried to snatch his hat off his head. He grabbed it impatiently, cramming it down. 'And there's nothing wrong with my gun hand.'

'I'm not arguing with you there,' Matt replied patiently, letting his chair tilt back against the wall. 'But it's only been four weeks, and that shoulder's not right. When you ride out of here you need to be fit, not held together with Laura's fancy bandages and a handful of bull-headed grit.'

'Then wait for me,' the cowboy begged. 'I'll be ready to ride in a week.'

'Laura doesn't agree,' Matt said. 'I figured you and she—'

'I ain't tied to no woman's skirts, not even hers,' Monty said impatiently. 'Look, Matt, she knows I'll be leaving. She knows there's things to do before I can think of settling down. You and me need to get started.'

'I'm going to Kansas, not Jeopardy.' Matt pointed to the chair alongside his own. 'Sit down before you fall down. I swear, Monty, I won't go back without you, I know how you feel about Logan.'

Monty scowled, but he slumped into the chair. 'Yeah, I guess you do. But that ain't what's bugging me. I got nothing to do here but think. An' all the time I come back to the same damn thing. It was all my fault. Jed would've listened to you. If I'd had more sense he'd still be alive.'

Matt sighed. 'Sure. And if I'd somehow kept Billy from

121

getting shot, or had the guts to arrest Logan for killing Mirabelle, it's likely a lot of good men would still be alive. It won't help, beating yourself over the head with your mistakes. We all make 'em. What's done is done. Soon as Ches gets back from Dewsburg I'll ride in and catch the train. When I get back, if you're fit and I've got what I need from the marshals, then we'll go looking for Logan.'

'Suppose Ches don't find out where Roper and O'Malley are?'

'Then I'll take my chance.' Matt fingered the growth of beard on his chin. 'What with this and Ches's Sunday suit I don't reckon anybody will know me. You just fix your mind on getting your strength back.'

A grating sound made itself heard above the wailing of the wind, making the men look up. Two bare feet showed over the edge of the roof, then Roy Trent dropped heavily to the ground, rolling over as his legs gave way beneath him. Before the men could move, the boy was up, turning to face Monty, his face red with anger. 'Don't you listen to him,' the boy said furiously, 'he's just yellow.' He shot a venomous look in Matt's direction. 'If he wasn't a coward my Pa wouldn't have died.'

'That ain't so,' Monty said.

'It is! He just said it! C'mon, Ricky, get down here.' Another pair of feet showed above their heads, and Matt rose swiftly to catch the younger Trent boy as he dropped.

'He heard it too,' Roy declared. 'Tell him, Ricky.'

Ricky pulled out of Matt's hands and retreated to the middle of the yard, where he had to brace himself against the wind, rising now to a deafening gale. He stood watching his brother warily, small fists clenched.

'Tell him!' Roy yelled.

'Leave him be,' Monty said. 'I'm the one who was

wrong, Roy, not Sheriff Turner. I never should've gone looking for Logan. And even if I was fit, which I ain't, I wouldn't go looking for him again, not without the sheriff's say so.'

The boy's face was contorted with fury. 'You're working for me now Ma and Pa are dead. An' I say you gotta go and kill Logan, Monty. Right now. I'll come with you.'

'Holy cow,' Matt breathed. 'That's just about all we need. Listen, kid—'

'Hey, you hear that?' Monty was on his feet, staring into the driven dust storm. 'Sounded like gunfire.'

'There's a horse coming.'

The sound of hoofbeats was just audible above the shrieking of the wind. Somebody was riding in fast. Matt leapt from his seat and ran to take a look, eyes smarting as they filled with grit.

The shadowy shape gradually became Ches Marryat, galloping towards them through the dust storm, his heels beating his horse's sides at every stride. 'Trouble,' the rancher gasped, jumping from the saddle and dragging his rifle from its holster. 'Two men on my heels. They know you're here, Matt.'

Even as he spoke a gun barked, and a shot whistled past Ches's head to bury itself in the wall of the barn.

Matt flung himself across the yard and swept up Ricky Trent, flinging the kid into Monty's hands.

'Get them inside,' he yelled, drawing his .45 and spinning the cylinder to check it was loaded as he ran, hurling himself towards the ranch house. Another shot ploughed a furrow in the dirt by Ches's feet. The rancher dived for cover behind the log pile, while his horse squealed and took off, reins trailing.

Sliding the gun back into its holster, Matt leapt to get

one foot on the side of the water trough, the other stepping on the hitching rail, his arms flailing as he reached
for the roof. He hauled himself up just as the first rider
came pounding into sight, a short-barrelled carbine in his
hands.

A bullet thudded into the wood only inches from Matt's
head as he hurled himself over the pitched roof, his left
hand hooking to stop him sliding off the other side. Then
the .45 was back in his hand, and he sent a couple of shots
in the rider's direction. The second grazed the gunman's
arm, not doing much damage, but spoiling his aim.
Cursing, the rider heaved on his mount's mouth, eager to
remove himself from Matt's line of fire.

'Look out, Matt!' Monty's urgent call came too late.
Seeing his partner was under fire, the second attacker had
turned away, to ride around the back of the house. Matt
grunted as he felt a shock shiver through his leg. He lost
his grip, the wind threatening to pluck him off the roof.
Matt tried to roll, to present a moving target without
falling, but the slope was too steep and he began to slide.
Sighting along the .45 as he slithered helplessly down the
shingles, he squeezed the trigger, but his shot sped harmlessly past the mounted man, and suddenly there was no
time to try again.

The blast of a shotgun deafened Matt as he slid off the
roof, and he caught a glimpse of the stranger's face in the
split second before it vanished in a spatter of bright red
blood. The cluster of lead shot had embedded itself in the
rider's throat, and the man tipped over in the saddle, the
horse shying when the hold on the rein slackened. As the
animal took flight, the body slumped and fell, landing
bonelessly by the corral fence.

Matt hit the ground hard, the air driven from his lungs

as he landed, his head cracking back against the rock-hard dirt. The man who'd taken the first shot at him reappeared. He'd come right around the cluster of buildings to come from behind the bunkhouse. Matt found himself staring into the barrel of the carbine. Even the wind seemed to be still, though dust still danced before his eyes. He looked death in the face and felt nothing but fury. He had sworn to make Logan pay for what he'd done to Two Shots. And Martha Trent had given her two sons into his care.

The gunshot sounded strangely muffled. As Matt dragged a breath into his aching lungs he realized the blast of the shotgun must have deafened him. That should have been his last thought, but the gunman seemed to slide away, vanishing from his sight. Then suddenly Ches was leaning over him instead, a smoking rifle in his hands.

'You all right?'

Still fighting for air, Matt could only nod. He knew he'd been hit as he lay on the roof, he'd felt the shock run through his body, but apart from his ribs, twinging painfully with each breath, nothing seemed to hurt.

'They're both dead,' Monty said dispassionately, coming to stand alongside Ches and breaking open Matt's shotgun, 'in case you was wonderin'. Don't neither of 'em look like Logan's men. Never saw 'em before.'

Matt rolled over and got to his hands and knees, air whooping into his chest. He could see the man Ches had killed, lying only a few feet away. There was something familiar about him, but this man hadn't ridden on Logan's so-called posse, and he was sure he'd never seen him in Jeopardy.

'Tubs Trendle,' Ches said. 'I sure am sorry, Matt.' He pulled a piece of paper from his vest pocket. 'He saw me looking at this. Guess he put two and two together. Wasn't more'n four miles out of Dewsburg before the pair of them got on my tail.'

He gave the paper to Matt. The picture was one that had appeared in the *County Star* a few years ago, when Matt tracked down a gang of train robbers. But this was no vale-dictory. Below the picture, the notice read: $500 REWARD. WANTED DEAD OR ALIVE *One time lawman Matt Turner is wanted for the cold-blooded murder of Deputy Sancho Mendez. He is also implicated in the death of Jedediah Whittaker, killed in a fire at the Blue Diamond Saloon in Jeopardy.*

'Trendle.' Matt nodded, then winced and was still as hammer blows began inside his head. 'He had that two-bit gambling house in Dewsburg.'

'Still does,' Ches said. 'But he earns more money out of bounty hunting these days. The other one's his cousin, name of Nathan. Been with him quite a while now. Pair of no-good lowlifes. One good thing: they won't have told anybody else where they were headed, too damn mean. Lucky, huh?'

Betsy was at Matt's side now, trying to make him lie back down. Waving her away, he pulled off his left boot and turned it over. Nathan Trendle's bullet had hit the heel. Putting his hand down inside the boot he could just feel it, a slight hard lump beneath his fingers. Matt grinned. 'That's what I call luck.'

Two pale faces appeared round the side of the bunkhouse. 'Hey,' Monty called harshly. 'Roy, come here.' He grabbed the boy by the shoulder and pulled him close to the man Ches had killed. 'Take a good look.'

Laura was at his side, her hand on the cowboy's arm. 'Monty, he's a child!' she protested.

'He reckons he's man enough to call Matt here a

coward. I just want him to see what happens when men bite off more'n they can chew. Two against three, kid. And that's what they get. Logan will have six men at his back, maybe more. You still want me an' the sheriff to ride straight back to Jeopardy?'

The boy was silent, staring at the dead man. Then he turned his gaze to Matt, still sitting on the ground, one hand massaging the back of his head. 'What about my pa? And Jed?' Roy was suddenly a child again, his voice wavering, a hint of dampness in his eyes. 'How are you going to make it right?'

'Only way I know,' Matt replied. 'By using the power of the law.'

'Could be difficult,' Ches put in, 'seeing Logan's been sending these posters to every lawman in four states.'

'You're sure nobody else knows I'm here?' Matt was pacing the distance from the water trough to the barn and back; but for the wind that still sent the dust swirling from every step, he would have worn a path.

'Trendle was watching me when I went to the sheriff's office. Maybe he even saw me pick up the poster.' Ches stood on the veranda, watching his friend's restless pacing. The two bodies had been dragged out of sight. 'He must've figured it out then; he's the kind would keep a grudge for a lifetime, and he never took kindly to the way we threw him off the Rocking M all those years ago.'

'Trying his hand at a little rustling, if I recall it right,' Matt said. 'Fact is, Ches, if he could work it out, then there's bound to be others thinking the same.' He scrunched the wanted poster in his fist. 'This changes things, I have to leave right now. We'll clear up, make sure there's no sign those two ever came here. I'll take their

127

horses with me, cut them loose when I'm twenty miles away.'

'You still plan to use the train?'

Matt sighed. 'Best not, I guess. Looks like I'll be wearing a few more blisters on my backside. How did you get on with the rest of the business in town?'

Ches felt in his pocket and drew out a handful of papers. 'I did what you wanted, I saw Arthur. You don't have to worry,' he went on, seeing Matt's face, 'I'd trust Arthur with my last nickel, even if he is a lawyer. He said he'll register the boys' claim through a friend of his. Coulter won't know where it came from. And he won't be able to claim the Circle T, seeing you and Monty will be legally responsible for the ranch until Roy's old enough to take over.'

'Good job we put Monty down as well. Until I clear my name Coulter could probably get a ruling against me.'

Abandoning his pacing, Matt headed into the barn and came out carrying two spades. 'Come on, let's dig a hole. Any ideas where the ground might be a bit softer?'

'Ought to just leave them for the coyotes,' Ches grumbled. 'We'll take a little walk, maybe try over by the fence. I don't want that pair of rattlesnakes buried too close to the house.'

CHAPTER THIRTEEN

Kurt Jensen woke to find something pressing on his nose and mouth; it smelt like mouldy leather. He froze, unable to make a sound, unable even to breathe. His first coherent thought was that he shouldn't have argued with Duke about the rebuilding of the Blue Diamond. Anger rose in his throat to replace that first instinctive fear. He forced his jaws apart and bit down hard.

His attack was rewarded by the sound of a muffled yelp, then a hushed voice speaking close to his ear. 'Hey, was that necessary? That's no way to greet an old friend.' The hand was slowly removed from his face.

'Dammit, there was no need to suffocate me!' Kurt spluttered.

'Sorry, can't see too well in the dark. Hush up will you, there's still folks hanging round, back of the saloon. I thought maybe they'd keep more civilized hours now they're under canvas.'

'Matt?' Kurt obediently dropped his voice to a whisper. 'That really you?'

'It was me last time I looked in the mirror, but that was quite a while ago,' the familiar voice replied.

Kurt chuckled. 'Hold on, give me a minute and I'll

check.' There were scuffling noises, and a few moments later Jensen lit the lamp. Jeopardy's one-time sheriff looked pretty much the same as ever, apart from a good growth of beard and a few more lines on his face. 'Sure is good to see you, Matt, but you shouldn't be here. Logan's got his boys out; there was a message came that you'd been seen near the Circle T a couple of days ago. That reminds me, how's Monty?'

'He's mending. Don't worry about Logan, Kurt, the men he's got watching the trail won't know I was here. But there's things I need to know, and you're the only one I can trust. Reckon Jeopardy has changed some.'

'Not for the better,' Jensen affirmed. 'You want some coffee?'

'Thanks,' Matt nodded. 'But keep it quiet. Sounds like there's still a party going on next door.'

'Duke's celebrating,' Kurt said. 'First part of the new saloon is up so they'll be taking the tent down in a couple of weeks.'

'Yeah, I saw all that timber in your yard. Sure am glad I didn't burn you out too, I felt bad about risking your place along with the Blue Diamond, but I didn't have much choice.'

'Reckon it won't make no never-mind anyhow,' Kurt said, handing Matt his coffee. 'Don't figure I'll be here much longer, Duke's new saloon is gonna be a whole lot bigger. Came round here a few days ago saying he wanted to buy my back yard. Be surprised if he stops there though, my place would give him all this side of Main Street.'

'Dammit! Hold on if you can, Kurt. Duke's going to be settling his accounts one day, but it's taking me a time.' Matt frowned. 'Logan's been real busy with his wanted posters. I've had trouble shaking off the bounty hunters.'

'The world's gone mad when a man like you is being hunted by the law.' Jensen was at the stove, picking up a pan. 'You hungry?'

'Yeah, but I don't have much time. Listen, Kurt, can you get hold of Sally Schott for me?'

Kurt made a sour face. 'Sure, but why?'

'There's things I need to ask her.' Matt glanced at the door as a gale of drunken laughter reached a crescendo in the street outside.

'Chances are she's right there,' Kurt said. 'You can ask your questions, but I wouldn't pin your hopes on getting a sensible answer. Sally took to the bottle in a big way right after that fire.'

'Is that so?' Matt nodded thoughtfully. 'Reckon she knew I was telling her the truth! Go on, Kurt, see if you can get her in here, but make it discreet.'

'I'll make it discreet all right,' Kurt grumbled. 'A man of my standing don't want to be seen dragging a woman like that into his home in the middle of the night. What d'you want her for?'

'Because she knows a lot about Duke. And because she can put a rope round Logan's neck if she tells the truth about what happened to Mirabelle.'

'I told you she'd be too far gone,' Kurt said disgustedly, heaving a barely conscious Sally Schott through the door. 'She won't be sober for hours. And I don't want her throwing up on my floor.'

'Here, black coffee,' Matt said, bringing a cup. 'The way you brew it, this stuff would get a dead horse back on its feet.'

It took two hours, and Matt was keeping an anxious eye on the sky outside the window by the time Sally looked at

131

him with something like comprehension in her eyes. He wanted to be clear of the town before daylight.

'You're a damn fool,' the woman said, her words only slightly slurred.

'Then that makes two of us,' Matt replied evenly, leaning over her as she slumped in Kurt Jensen's rocking chair. 'How come you let Coulter fool you that way?'

'What are you talking about?' She ran a tongue over her lips. 'Sure am dry. You got anything to drink?'

'Coffee,' Matt offered, lifting the cup.

'Hell, no. That stuff tastes like creosote. I need a real drink.'

'Not till we've finished talking. Get the lady some water, Kurt.'

Sally pushed the proffered glass away. 'I got nothing to say to you, Turner. Except that you're a crazy fool, coming back to Jeopardy. Seeing as you called me a lady I won't tell Duke you were here, but you'd better split, and fast.'

'I'll go, soon as I'm done talking. I went to Serena, Sally, and spoke to a few folks there. Seems it wasn't exactly your idea giving up that place of yours.'

'That skunk Herb Dornvill!' She spat the words at Matt and he recoiled from the powerful waft of alcohol that came with them. 'He bought out my lease, right under my nose, then he helped those prissy women and that tame preacher of theirs to run me out of town!'

'It wasn't Herb,' Matt said. 'Oh, sure, he moved the deal along, but it wasn't his idea. He didn't have much choice once Logan started leaning on him. Didn't you notice how Duke popped up so conveniently to offer you a job, when you had to make a move?'

'Duke?' Sally's drink-sodden mind was gradually clearing, but it was working slow. 'You say Duke was the one?'

Matt nodded. 'He had an eye on your daughter.'

At this she sat bolt upright, a hand reaching to grab the front of his shirt. 'Who told you about Mirabelle? How d'you know? The girl didn't even look like me. That sweet little schoolmarm look of hers, had 'em all fooled. And I brought her up right. She was saving herself for a decent man, a man with some money and a proper home.'

'You were close to getting it for her, weren't you? Until you were forced out of Serena.'

Sally nodded, tears beginning to dampen the powder on her raddled face. 'She wasn't supposed to end up that way,' she whispered. 'She was gonna have everything I never had.'

'Drowning yourself in whiskey won't make you feel any better,' Matt told her. 'Why don't you help me? Make the man who killed Mirabelle pay for his crime.'

'Duke swore I'd got it wrong. He swore it was the kid.' She wiped the tears away, her face hardening. 'Maybe it's you that's lying. How do I know you're tellin' the truth about Herb?'

'Don't take my word for it. Send somebody you trust to Serena; the talk's all over town.'

The woman stared up at Matt, the muscles around her mouth suddenly sagging. 'Ain't no need.' Her eyes were no longer seeing him and she was silent for a long moment, her thoughts turned inward. 'What do you want me to do?'

'Stand up in court when I bring Logan and Coulter to trial,' Matt said promptly. 'Stand up and tell the truth. You do that and Herb Dornvill's gonna do the same. He wants you back, Sally, reckons Serena's not the same without you. Get rid of Duke and he'll cut you a good deal.'

*

Two men rode side by side along the road that ran out of Kansas and headed west. One was getting along in years, with grizzled hair and a face that spoke of many summers, though he sat straight and easy in the saddle. The other was young enough to be his son, though there was no resemblance between them. Each wore a badge pinned on his vest, and a six-gun tied down at his side.

From his hiding place behind the crumbling walls of an abandoned cabin, Matt watched them come, one hand over the bay's nose to keep the horse silent. His heart was beating uncomfortably fast. By law these men had the right, no, more than the right, the *duty*, to shoot him down in cold blood. He was betting his freedom, maybe even his life, on an old friendship, and he chewed on his lip as the two riders approached, the older man saying something that brought a laugh from the youngster.

Drawing in a deep breath, Matt stepped out of cover, moving from the deep shade of the cabin's lopsided roof into the brightness of the sun, low in the sky now as the days grew shorter.

'Howdy, Jay. Marshal Dobson.' He held his hands wide, showing himself unarmed. 'Glad to see you're both back in the saddle.'

The two marshals spurred their horses, coming either side of him. Dobson scowled, his hand on the butt of his six-gun. 'You giving yourself up, Turner? Would've been easier to ride into town.'

'Hold on, Bert,' Jay said, leaning forward to rest his forearms on his saddlebow. 'This here fella's got a beard. Kinda hard to see exactly what he'd look like without it, so I don't reckon we can be sure this is Turner. Don't look one scrap like that picture the sheriff of Jeopardy's got posted all the way from Montana to Missouri. An' that's another thing: we had reports that fugitive's been seen heading for Canada.' The marshal gave a lopsided smile. 'That's when he ain't holed up in the badlands along with the Idaho Kid an' Soupy Joe.'

Matt grinned. 'Sure makes my life hard, the way folks keep mistaking me for that renegade lawman. I hear he's wanted for two murders.'

'Last I heard it was five,' Jay Brand said. He turned to Dobson, whose scowl had transformed itself to puzzlement. 'Tell you what, Bert, why don't you ride on to the way-station, same as we planned, and I'll join you real soon. No need to tell anyone what's holding me up here, I'll be along real soon.'

'If you say so, Marshal.'

'I do say so. Now git.'

Still the youngster lingered, his eyes never leaving Matt's face. 'Listen, kid,' Marshal Brand said, pushing his horse forward so it came between the two men, 'if you see Matt Turner, you have to run him in, right?'

Dobson nodded.

'Well, in that case,' Brand went on patiently, 'you haven't seen him. Because if you think I'm going to send an old friend to a neck-tie party on the say-so of a pair of crooks like Duke Coulter and that murderous hired gun of his, then you don't know me too well.'

There was a moment's charged silence. 'I know you,' Dobson replied at last. 'And I got reason enough to trust you. Don't reckon we owe nothing to the sheriff of Jeopardy, the way he nigh on ran us out of town a few weeks back. Figure I'll stay and hear what this stranger's got to say.' He eased down from the saddle. 'Reckon it's about time we brewed some coffee, must be close to noon.'

Matt looked questioningly at Brand, who gave a shrug before stepping down from his horse. 'The boy's got a mind of his own,' he said, by way of apology. 'Ain't a lot an old man like me can do about it.'

'Three heads could be better than two,' Matt said. 'I'm going to need all the help I can get.'

Summer was a distant memory. The wind howled around the slow-moving freight car, blasts of icy air finding their way through cracks in the slatted sides. Two hobos sat hunched in a corner, filthy old hats pulled low.

'You'd better be right this time,' the older man grumbled, trying to hug his arms more tightly against his sides. His beard and hair were long and tangled, more grey than brown, and he flexed his right hand, making a fist then stretching the fingers out, doing it over and over as if the movement was an unconscious habit.

'Red Bluff Junction,' the younger hobo said, his voice muffled because his head was sunk so low into his ragged coat. 'But if this damn train don't get a move on we'll miss him. That's if we don't freeze to death first.' As if in response the car jolted then began to pick up speed. He got up and heaved the sliding door open an inch, peering out into the growing gloom. 'The snow's holding off, reckon maybe our luck's changing.' He was much younger than his companion, and might have been thought good-looking, but for the still vivid scars on his cheek and jaw-line, and the way his nose had recently set crooked.

'About time.' The older man looked up as the train lurched and the younger hobo staggered, grimacing as he flung out a hand to keep himself from falling. 'You all right?'

'I'm fine. Looks like we'll be there in a few minutes.

Can you move, or are you frozen to them planks?'

By way of answer Matt Turner hauled himself upright and stamped his feet, flailing his arms. 'Give you a licking any day,' he said, taking his turn at the open door. 'Best get out before we stop; the brakeman'll be searching these wagons soon as we reach the depot.' He sent a worried look in Monty Caine's direction. 'Can you jump?' The boy had healed, but he could have used another month to completely recover from the beating Logan's men had inflicted.

'Will you quit fussing?' Monty grinned. 'Hell, you're worse than Laura. I can jump a whole lot better than an old has-been like you.'

Matt let that pass, checking that his gunbelt was well hidden beneath his overlarge coat, bought the night before from a tramp who had shared their draughty accommodation for a few hours.

Red Bluff had a railroad depot, and not much else. 'There' – Monty was triumphant – 'I told you!' A single passenger car was being attached to a locomotive, light spilling out from under the blinds covering the windows. Behind the car was a caboose with no lights showing. 'We got him this time!'

It was almost full dark now, and nobody noticed the two ragged men leaping on to the steps at the back of the passenger car as the train started down the line, ahead of the freight, which had stopped to take on fuel and water. They crouched low, though on such a bitter night nobody was fool enough to be out and about unless they had to, so the risk of them being spotted was small.

'Careful,' Matt cautioned, keeping his voice low. The surface beneath them was slick with frozen snow and even the handrail alongside the steps had an icy covering. 'Be real easy to slide right off here.'

Monty nodded, keeping a firm grip as he edged closer to the covered window to peer through the gap beneath the blind. 'We got him,' he said again. 'And he's all alone.'

'Maybe, but there's a vestibule at the other end of the car. And why put this thing on the train if nobody's using it?' Matt stepped warily across the gap and quietly tried the door of the caboose. It was locked. 'Wherever you find Roper that ape O'Malley's never far away.'

'Not always. O'Malley was at the Blue Diamond that night, but I didn't see Roper.'

'Best expect some kind of trouble.' Matt shivered, it was getting colder. 'We'll wait a while. Make our move once we're a couple of miles out.'

'Nobody with any sense is going to be outside tonight.' Monty hunkered down, getting what shelter he could from the end of the passenger car. 'I thought it was cold in that damn freight train, but if we stay here too long we'll be frozen where we stand.'

The locomotive's whistle blew a mournful note as they left the outskirts of Red Bluff behind. When there was nothing to be seen behind the train but the cold dark, Matt stood up, anchoring his feet as best he could on the slippery surface. As if at a signal the snow began to fall at that moment, thick and fast, driven sideways by the wind.

Flexing his shoulders and swinging his arms a time or two to get the circulation going, Matt had to fight to stay upright in the sudden blizzard. He motioned Monty to open the door into the car. 'Follow me in.'

Matt barrelled in. Taken by surprise Roper sat frozen in his comfortable chair, a glass of whiskey halfway to his lips. Recovering himself before Matt reached him the railroad man came swiftly to his feet, turning to run and shouting as he went. 'O'Malley! Get in here!'

Matt jerked Roper to him, silencing him with a swift chop of his hand to the man's throat, but the damage had been done. As Roper fell choking to the floor, the door at the end of the car opened and a huge figure came rushing through. Matt glanced back, hoping to see Monty coming to help him, baffled when he found he was alone. There wasn't time to run, and nowhere to run to. He turned back to face the onslaught, feeling like a pup caught in a pen with a maddened bull.

CHAPTER FOURTEEN

In the split second before O'Malley's full weight struck him, Matt let himself fall backwards. O'Malley had been moving too fast to stop, and he came toppling, one nailed boot scoring across Matt's shin, arms flailing. Matt grunted in pain, but he already had the other leg raised, and aiming with deadly accuracy, he put all his strength behind a hefty kick. The big man's squeal of agony as the blow struck him between the legs told Matt he'd found his target, and he rolled to get out of the way as the massive body crashed to the floor.

Matt rose swiftly to his feet. O'Malley was clutching at his crotch and rolling in agony. His eyes, filled with pain and fury, were fixed on Matt's face. Matt was breathing hard already though the fight had barely started. Back down the car there was still no sign of Monty. Chewing on his lip, Matt wondered if the cowboy had slipped on the ice and fallen off the train. Even if he'd survived the fall and not died under the wheels, he wouldn't last long out in the blizzard with no shelter nearer than Red Bluff.

While Matt hesitated, O'Malley was struggling to his feet. The giant's face was twisted into an expression of pure hatred, and Matt knew he had no choice. It was kill or be killed; there was nowhere to go unless he jumped off the train into the freezing night. Matt hadn't come all this way, working for weeks to track Roper down and catch him alone, just to give up now. He spared a brief thought for Monty, but, dead or alive, there was nothing he could do for the cowboy, except maybe pay O'Malley back for that beating in the Blue Diamond.

Matt gritted his teeth. It was time to put aside his scruples and forget about fair play. He fumbled for the six-gun hidden under his hobo's coat, swearing at his stupidity; he should have taken the damn thing off before he came rushing into the car. Now his groping fingers tangled in the torn lining, and the gun wouldn't come free.

O'Malley was advancing on him, slowly, taking his time. His lips lifted slowly in a savage grin as he realized he had Matt trapped.

Matt had finally located the .45, but although he had his fingers wrapped around the butt it was held fast. Try as he might, he couldn't even turn it around and shoot at O'Malley through the cloth. Cursing, he gave up on the gun and faced the big man again, lifting clenched fists; his opponent had muscle but he was short on intelligence. It was brains against brawn; it had to be possible to out-think this brute.

This time O'Malley moved slow, all the while driving Matt into a corner. Walking backwards, one careful step at a time, Matt knocked against a chair. He reached to pick up this welcome weapon, pleased to find it was heavy. A sudden movement alongside caught his eye; he'd forgotten about Roper. Luckily the man was no threat. He was

141

cowering against the side of the car, intent only on keeping out of the way.

Seeing Roper gave Matt an idea. He might still survive. Out in the open he could maybe make use of the storm, or at least he might gain a breathing space, win a little time and try for his gun again.

Matt threw the chair at O'Malley's head. The big man swatted it away without breaking stride, his grin broadening as the chair smashed against the side of the car, two legs splintering, but Matt made the most of the diversion. He lunged across to where Roper stood and pulled him into a rough embrace, keeping the railroad boss moving, sending him spinning around then giving him a violent shove that tumbled him into O'Malley's arms.

There was a split second to spare, and a couple of feet of vacant space as O'Malley sought to disentangle himself, and Matt didn't waste them. He darted past the two men, leaping over the ruins of the chair and sprinting for the other end of the car, heading for the door that stood open, the freezing air hitting him when he was still feet away. As he ran Matt plucked at the voluminous coat, intent on ridding himself of it.

He was two strides from the door when he finally learned why Monty never made it into the car. The caboose hadn't been empty after all. Two figures reeled across the icy veranda. They were locked together in a wrestling hold, their feet sliding on the metal plates as each of them attempted to throw the other off the train. The locomotive had picked up speed and the car was rocking energetically from side to side, making their struggle all the more precarious.

The snow was being driven against the combatants by the howling wind, and their clothes gleamed white. It looked like Monty was getting the worst of the match; Matt had been right, the cowboy wasn't fully recovered and his adversary was pressing him hard. It was Grice, the engineer Jed Whittaker had downed back at the Blue Diamond a lifetime ago.

Matt wanted to go to Monty's aid, but he had troubles of his own. Slowed down by his tussle with the coat, he could hear O'Malley's heavy breathing as the big man lunged after him. Finally flinging the heavy garment down, Matt reached for his gun. But before he could draw, before he'd even reached the doorway, a massive paw took hold of his right shoulder, squeezing flesh and bone in a vicelike grip. While his hand was mending Matt had learnt to use his left, but his gunbelt had hitched itself around behind his right buttock while he fought with the coat, and he couldn't reach the .45.

Unable to see his next move, Matt's mind was doing cartwheels, coming up with nothing. The giant could deliver a single killing stroke to the back of his neck, and he'd be finished. But the blow didn't come. The big man was merely holding him, preventing him from reaching the door. Matt groped left-handed in the pocket of his vest, locating the canvas-wrapped bundle hidden there and pulling it free.

O'Malley laughed, and that was when Matt knew he still had a chance of survival. The brute enjoyed inflicting pain. Just killing Matt wouldn't be enough. There was that kick Matt had given him too: it was payback time. O'Malley was trying to pull Matt around. He wanted to see his victim's face before he pummelled him to a pulp.

His arm going numb under the pressure on his shoulder, Matt's lips curled in an icy smile. That cruel streak would give him the edge he needed. He closed his fingers tighter on the secret weapon he'd used so effectively on Monty Caine.

But then everything changed. Outside on the veranda Monty was falling, his body striking the metal floor with a solid thud. Grice had one arm around the handrail, his other hand going to a sheath at his waist. A blade caught the lamplight spilling from the car, yellow among the glistening whiteness of the snow.

Desperation lending him a strength he didn't know he had, Matt lunged for the door, heaving O'Malley bodily along behind him. It was only two paces but it seemed like ten times that. It felt to Matt as if he was single-handedly dragging the train up a steep hill.

By some miracle he was in time. Matt chopped down at Grice's neck with the makeshift blackjack. The railroad engineer grunted and dropped like a stone. The knife fell from the man's unconscious hand, bounced off the metal deck and vanished into the night.

Despite O'Malley's fingers still maintaining their grip and grinding into him, Matt fell across the engineer's body, unable to keep his feet. At last his shoulder tore free from O'Malley's grasp, though it felt to Matt as if he'd left a handful of flesh behind.

The wind had risen to a gale, and the snow was coming so thick and fast it was impossible even to see the caboose across the three foot gap. Matt tried to push upright, but his hands and feet slid away from beneath him and the wind was pushing him sideways. His head was out over the steps, and he glimpsed gleaming metal where the rails rushed by below.

The train was travelling fast, to fall would be to die. Matt had only a second to save himself before the gale and the motion shook him free. He could get no purchase on the icy metal. As if that wasn't enough, somewhere behind him there was O'Malley.

Blinded by the swirling snow, Matt couldn't see the strut that supported the handrail, but it had to be there. He flung out his arm, his wrist making painful contact. Biting down on a yell, he threw his other arm across. His body slid off the platform, and he hit the steps hard, but he had both arms clamped around the upright, and he clung on in a desperate embrace.

Through the swirling snow two dark shapes emerged, only inches from Matt's face. O'Malley's boots. The giant leaned down and laughed at him, his huge body swaying with the motion of the train. He took hold of the rail to steady himself, then with slow deliberation he stamped on Matt's arms. Matt gritted his teeth against the pain; death was only moments away.

To his dying day, Matt would never know why O'Malley loosed his hold on the handrail. Maybe he was frustrated by Matt's refusal to let go, or by his inability to reach Matt's hands; finger bones would have broken far quicker under the assault from his boots. Or maybe he was going to pull Matt back on to the platform, not wanting his victim to die so soon.

The reason didn't matter. O'Malley's feet began to slide on the frozen snow, and he flung his hand out to take a grip. But some force, stronger even than the wind, thrust hard against his back. Arms windmilling, the huge body soared over Matt's head.

O'Malley was gone, leaving nothing but a faint cry behind him, the sound torn into shreds in an instant and lost in the shriek of the wind. For Matt the big man's death had come almost too late. The cold was creeping deeper, a vice squeezing ever tighter against every part of his body.

He could almost feel his blood freezing in his veins. The frozen snow, hard slivers of ice driven by the wind, was flaying skin from his face, but he was no longer aware of it.

Matt made one feeble effort to lift a foot on to the steps, but he no longer had the strength. His arms were still locked into place, keeping him alive, but it could only be a matter of time. He was barely conscious when the hand wrapped itself round his arm. He was pulled up, dragged across the veranda and into the passenger car. Warm air struck him and he revived a little. There was a crash as the door was slammed shut, then for a few moments a void. The next he knew Matt was being rolled over, to see Monty peering anxiously into his face.

'Matt? You all right?'

Matt groaned. 'I'll live.' He turned his head and saw Grice lying alongside him. 'What about him?'

'Out cold. You did it again, Sheriff, and I still didn't see how.'

Not bothering to remind Monty that he was no longer a lawman, Matt sat up, looking at his hands. Blood was oozing from cracks in the flesh. 'I'll show you,' he said, 'but not right now.' The little canvas bag full of lead shot must be lying out in the snow somewhere, miles behind them. He peered down the passenger car. 'Where's Roper?'

'Sitting on the floor back there, like I told him.' Monty grinned, which only made his filthy bearded face, stippled now with frostbite, look even more villainous. 'I said he'd be joinin' O'Malley unless he behaved himself.'

Matt nodded, not surprised that Roper hadn't argued. 'Get Grice tied up; reckon he's got more guts than Roper.' He rose to his feet, staggering a little, and made his way to where the railroad boss cowered in a corner.

'Well, Mr Roper, you're a mighty hard man to pin down, but I reckon we can have a real good talk now, and there ain't a soul to interrupt us.'

The snow was knee-deep and still falling fast. Three men faced into the blizzard, two of them walking doggedly into the storm, the third being dragged bodily along between them. They were all wet to the skin, the cold penetrating deep, but only Roper was shivering, his teeth chattering so loud that Matt could hear them above the howl of the wind.

'Walk!' Matt yelled, leaning to shout in the smaller man's ear. 'Dammit, use your legs and you won't feel the cold so bad.'

'This is madness!' Instead of obeying, Roper pulled free, raising his voice to make himself heard. 'Our only hope is to follow the tracks, we have to go back. It was insane, leaving the train on a night like this.'

Monty Caine's hand shot out and he grabbed Roper, his other fist lifting.

'No.' Matt stepped between the cowboy and the rail-road man, making Monty relinquish his hold.

'Aw, come on, Matt.' Monty turned to face Matt, spitting fresh snow out of his mouth. 'He's driving me crazy. Hell, it's worse'n havin' a woman along. Just one little plug to shut that miserable mouth of his. I swear I won't knock him cold or nothing.'

Roper was backing away. 'I'm going,' he said. 'I'll walk along the line.'

'Do that and you're a dead man,' Matt said patiently. 'There won't be any more trains tonight, and by dawn you'll be frozen solid.'

'We'll all be dead if we go on! There's no way you can

147

find your way through this blizzard: you can't see more than a yard in front of your feet.'

'No need. We got off that train exactly where I planned. We're heading for something that's been there a whole lot longer than the railroad, and it's even harder to miss. Now come on, get moving, or maybe I'll let Monty give you that punch on the jaw.' Matt took a step towards Roper then stopped dead. The railroad man had pulled out a little silver-mounted revolver. He pointed it at Matt, his hand shaking.

'Keep away from me.'

'Well, darn,' Matt said, half amused. 'If you'd had the guts to use that while I was dealing with O'Malley, reckon none of us would be out here in the snow!'

'It's a real shame you need him, Matt,' Monty said. 'Sure wish we could just let him go. Don't figure he'd be any loss.'

'Maybe not, but, like you say, we need him. Come on, Roper, it ain't safe to play around with guns. Put that away and get walking, before we all freeze to death.'

Instead of obeying, Roper tightened his grip, the gun waving wildly as he pulled the trigger. Although Matt was standing almost within arm's reach of him the shot missed him by a foot. Behind him he heard Monty give a yelp of surprise.

'He shot me! That little skunk just shot me!' The cowboy came barrelling past Matt, one hand batting the gun from Roper's fingers, the other taking hold of the railroad man by the back of his neck. 'I been holding off, seeing Matt's got this idea about keeping to the law, but so help me, I've been wanting to detach your head from your body ever since we got on that train. You and Coulter, you're two of a kind, hiding behind scum like O'Malley

148

an' Logan, pretending to be decent law-abiding citizens while them animals do the dirty work. You're yellow as a prairie dog, Roper, an' just this once you're getting what's comin' to you.' He shoved Matt aside as the older man tried to intervene, and landed a full-bodied punch on the side of Roper's head.

Roper went down without a sound, and lay still.

'Dammit, if you've killed him . . .' Matt said furiously, bending over Roper's body.

'He ain't dead. But it's nothing but luck that slug only grazed my leg.' Monty picked Roper up and slung him over his shoulder, striding away. 'Come on. An' I'm about sick of this damn snow, so you'd better be right about finding the river.'

'Keep going at that speed and you'll be swimming in it any time now,' Matt replied. 'You maybe didn't notice the way we've been going downhill.'

'Fine.' Monty stopped and faced him. 'So now what?'

'There.' Matt pointed to his right. A dim patch of yellow lamplight showed in the swirling whiteness. With a grunt Monty shouldered past him.

'Come on in.' Ches Marryat stood in the doorway of the cabin. 'Thought I heard you coming. In fact, I thought I heard a shot.' He stared at Roper as Monty flung him down on the floor. 'Is he dead?'

'No, just needs thawing out some,' Monty replied. 'I'm the one who got shot.' He took off a boot and pulled up the leg of his pants. The ball had barely nicked his flesh; there was only a trickle of blood just below his knee, already congealed.

'Nasty,' Ches said, straightfaced. 'Looks like this Roper's a real dangerous character.'

'It ain't funny,' Monty said, tugging his boot back on,

'that hole in my pants is letting in a powerful lot of cold air.'

'Coffee's hot,' Ches offered.

'Never mind the coffee,' Matt said, slamming the door shut behind him. 'Did you bring the horses?'

'Eight of 'em, just like you said. But the way it's snowing I reckon we'll be lucky to make it.'

'We'll make it.' Matt said grimly. 'I've waited long enough for this, and now we've got Roper talking we can nail Coulter, and the whole damn mess of 'em.'

CHAPTER FIFTEEN

Old drifts of snow were still banked up along Jeopardy's sidewalks, left there by the storm that had raged through the town a couple of weeks before. The day was cold although the sun shone from a clear sky, which may have accounted for the silence in the streets.

There was nobody to see the two men who came riding into town, their horses' hoofs sliding now and then on the icy ground. The man on the bay had grizzled hair and a wild tangle of beard. He rode straight-backed, looking neither to left or right. The younger man at his side wore a buffalo skin wrapped around his shoulders to keep out the cold. He sat his roan like the horse was a part of him; there were healing scars on his face and his nose was set crooked, but a woman might still think him handsome.

At that moment Monty Caine didn't have women on his mind.

'Of all the crazy things I ever did,' he muttered, 'this has to be the craziest.' He scanned the rooftops then glanced into Kurt Jensen's blacksmith shop. It appeared to be deserted, but he thought he saw movement deep in the shadows inside. 'What's to stop them gunning us down before we even get off our horses?'

'Pride,' Matt Turner replied. 'They'll want to see us beaten, count on it. And they'll want the town to see it too.'

'Sure hope you're right.' They were alongside the Blue Diamond, rebuilt twice the size of the previous one, and resplendent in new paint, with a name board across the front a clear five feet high.

A two-horse wagon stood right outside the saloon's door, and the two men swung around it before heading in to the hitching rail. 'Do better with a sled, the weather we've been having,' Matt remarked, stepping up on to the sidewalk, though he noticed the powerful shoulders and quarters of the two horses with approval. Monty didn't reply, throwing off the buffalo skin and draping it across his saddle. With a quick movement he made sure his six-gun moved smoothly from its holster before dropping it back into place.

'Take it easy,' Matt cautioned. 'We're not here to start anything, remember.' He pushed open the double doors and stepped inside.

'I remember,' Monty whispered as he followed him. 'But if they start it, I'll sure see it finished.'

Duke Coulter sat alone at a large circular table, an open bottle and three glasses before him, along with a single sheet of folded paper. 'Hello, Turner. I heard you were coming. Not the weather for travelling.'

'Coulter.' Matt nodded. 'A man can't let a bit of snow get in the way, not when he's got something important to do.'

'Of course. As it happens some of my boys just got back from a trip, too. I think you'll be interested in something they brought with them.' He glanced round, and there was Logan, standing at the top of the fancy new staircase,

152

twice as wide as the old one. Coulter jerked his head and the gunslinger turned and vanished through a doorway.

'You've had a chilly ride.' Coulter said, turning back to the two new arrivals. 'Would you like a drink?'

'No thanks,' Matt said shortly.

'No? How about you, Caine. Best whiskey I have. On the house, of course.'

'I'd sooner sign the pledge than drink with you.' Monty's voice was as cold as the frozen snow outside.

Coulter tutted. 'Now that's a shame. Figure a man ought to enjoy his last few moments. Sure I can't persuade you?' He poured himself a shot and tossed it back. 'Well, if you're not here for a drink then maybe you'd like to tell me what you're doing in my saloon.'

'We're here to arrest you.' Matt said.

Coulter threw back his head and laughed. 'That's got to be the funniest thing I ever heard. I'm about to be arrested by a washed-up old man who's on the run from the law, and a cowboy who keeps his brains in his fists!'

'Wrong,' Matt replied, unfastening his coat and holding it open to show the badge he wore. 'You're about to be arrested by two federal marshals, Coulter.'

A door opened upstairs, and Logan reappeared. He held a long-barrelleed Colt in his hand. 'You want them now, boss?'

Coulter nodded, smiling as he turned back to Matt. 'You didn't give me time to tell you about our guests,' he said smoothly. 'Bring them down, Logan, but slowly. We don't want any accidents.'

At a gesture from Logan two figures appeared and stepped out into the light.

'No!' Monty took a step forward, his hand going for his gun, but Matt slapped an urgent hand on his partner's arm. Betsy and Laura Badon came down the stairs side by side, heads held high. Logan came along behind, careful to keep the women between himself and the two men down below.

Laura looked pale and drawn, biting on her lip and avoiding Monty's eyes, but Betsy looked straight at Matt as she reached the bottom step, and her expression was serene. She held her hands just a little way from her body, palms downwards, each at a slightly different level, and gave a slight nod of her head.

Matt understood the gesture. Many times he'd seen her place her hands on the heads of the two Trent boys in exactly that way. He let out a long breath; it was bad that the two women were here, but at least the youngsters had escaped. Maybe Coulter still didn't know that Ches Marryat had taken them in.

'This is no place for ladies,' Matt said, keeping his voice under control though his heart was pounding.

'I agree. That's why the saloon is closed just now,' Coulter was all smooth, civilized good manners. He held out chairs and waited until the women were settled before he too took a seat. 'Won't you join us, Turner, Caine? You'll want to take those gunbelts off first.' It wasn't an invitation. Logan stood a couple of feet behind Betsy, his gun aimed unwaveringly at the back of her head. 'On that other table, thank you. Now, we need to talk about what happens next.'

'Let them go, Coulter,' Monty growled. 'You got us, and we're unarmed. You don't need these ladies any more.'

'Hmm.' Coulter pretended to think about it. 'I'm sorry, but I think maybe I do. You see, there's the matter of the Circle T. It seems you two gentlemen will need to sign a document for me, and I'm not sure even Logan here will be able to persuade you, unless we have a little bargaining power.'

Monty was halfway out of his seat, but Logan was quicker. He had Laura by the hair, jerking her head up and thrusting the Colt under her chin. There was an evil grin on his face. 'Personally I'd prefer a blade,' he said, 'but the boss here decided a bullet was quicker, more permanent. Hell, maybe it's even kinder, what d'you say, Caine?'

'There's no need for this,' Matt said. 'We'll give you what you want.'

'I thought you might.' Coulter unfolded the piece of paper. 'I'm sorry, I seem to have forgotten the writing materials.' As he stood up a woman came through the door from the back rooms.

The few weeks since Matt last saw her had done Sally Schott no favours. Her hair was coarse and untidy, her dress none too clean, and the powerful scent of stale whiskey wafted across the room as she came swaying over to the table. 'Something you want, Duke?' She tossed her head at the other two women. 'Bringin' the tone of the place down some, ain't you?'

'We need pen and ink, Sally. Bring them, then go.'

Ignoring his hostile tone the woman draped her arms around Coulter's neck and looked across the table at Matt. 'This new place is real fine, don't you think so, Sheriff? Best thing of all is them new lamps. Duke's so proud of them things, keeps 'em alight even when the sun's shining.' She waved a hand at the ceiling. 'See the way they're hung up so high? No roughhouse is gonna cause a fire in here, huh?' Pushing herself away from Duke she lurched back to the bar and reached to a metal peg on the wall. 'It's so smart, you just unhook this little bitty chain, an' down it comes.'

'Careful, Sally,' Coulter cautioned. 'Leave it alone. Look, just go and fetch the writing things, then you can have a drink.'

'I don't think so,' the woman replied. She had the lamp in her hands, and was swaying under the weight of it. 'You know, Duke, I never guessed about that deal you did with Herb Dornvill. See, I trusted you.' She removed the cap from the reservoir, and a little oil slopped out of the lamp on to the floor. Coulter rose to his feet in alarm.

'No, Sally. Listen, you've got it wrong. I wasn't—' He broke off, seeing the woman beginning to tip the lamp some more. 'Logan, stop her!'

Logan let go of Laura and raised the Colt.

'Not that, you fool!' Coulter yelled. 'If she drops it the whole place might burn!'

With a curse Logan holstered his gun and charged across the room. He had his arms outstretched to grab the lamp, his shoulder pitching into Sally and knocking her over. Logan didn't get a firm enough grip, and even as she fell, her head smashing hard against the bar, Sally jerked the lamp half out of his grasp before she let it go. Oil splashed Logan from head to foot, and the glass fell to the floor with a crash. The lighted wick barely touched the man's arm but with his clothes and hair doused in oil, Logan had no chance. Within a breath he was a human torch, screaming as he tried to beat out the flames.

Logan staggered towards the doorway, but he couldn't see. He lurched wildly into the shelf behind the bar, bringing a couple of bottles crashing down to add new fuel to the flames.

For a horrified moment the men and women around the table remained frozen in their places, then Matt was on his feet, grabbing Laura, who was closest to him, and pushing her at Monty. 'Out,' he said tersely. Monty obeyed, dragging Laura to the door. Matt took a step towards Betsy, then stopped dead. Coulter too had recovered from his shocked trance. He stood at Betsy's side, the sharp narrow blade of a stiletto held to her throat.

'Put out the fire, Turner,' Duke Coulter said wildly. 'Put it out, or say goodbye to your woman right now.'

Matt couldn't get close to Logan. A harrowing ululation of agony issued from the man's scorched throat as he reeled on burning feet, his blackened hands clawing uselessly at sightless eyes. Matt darted past him and opened the door which led outside, then he picked up a broom from behind the bar and pushed the column of burning flesh outside. Logan tottered and fell, landing in a drift of frozen snow. He rolled over just once before he lay still, the awful sound he'd been making finally silenced.

There was a bucket by the door. Matt scooped snow into it and ran back inside, dumping the first load around Sally Schott where she lay unconscious; only a solitary flame had found her, one side of her skirt was burnt away, but the layers of petticoats she wore looked to have saved her. By the time Matt came back with the second load of snow the woman was recovering, getting to hands and knees and crawling away from the fire.

Three more times Matt made the journey, coughing as smoke and steam rose from the smouldering floorboards, unable to see if the job was done as his eyes streamed. Sure at last that the fire was out Matt flung down the bucket and swiped his sleeve across his eyes. 'Now, Coulter . . .' he began, but the barroom was empty. The man had vanished, along with both Betsy and Sally Schott.

Matt ran back to the table where he and Monty had left

their firearms. The two holsters where there, but not the guns. He ran to fling open the doors. His and Monty's horses still stood where they'd left them, but the wagon had gone. A procession was coming along the street towards him. Ches Marryat, Kurt Jensen, Clive Pechey and Marshal Dobson walked behind four men, all of whom had their hands tied and their legs hobbled. Seeing Matt, Ches called across to him. 'Your friend Jay got two more, including Harve Rawlins. Monty's helping to bring 'em in. And there's one at the back of the livery who won't be needing the hangman. Reckon that's about it.'

'Except for Coulter,' Matt said. 'He didn't come out this way?'

Ches shook his head. 'You need help?'

'No,' Matt said bleakly, 'just a gun.'

The new stairs creaked beneath his boots. At the top Matt took Kurt's elderly .38 from the front of his belt, took a deep breath and threw open the door. As if at a signal a noise began, more dreadful in its way than Logan's dying wails. A woman was screaming.

His boots pounding out a desperate drumbeat, Matt hurled himself towards the terrible sound. A door stood open at the end of the passage and he raced through, the gun cocked and ready.

As he'd expected, Coulter was ready and waiting for him. It was Sally who was screaming. She knelt by the window, her body rocking back and forth. Her hands were clasped tightly over her face and there was blood seeping out from between her fingers.

Duke Coulter sat on a bed, with Betsy crouching on the floor at his feet. The stiletto he held must have pricked the side of her neck. A tiny red bead of blood stood out against the paleness of her flesh. The guns Matt and

Monty had left on the table downstairs lay on the coverlet, a couple of inches from Duke's other hand.

Without waiting to be told, Matt lowered the .38 to the floor, sending it sliding away from him. He held out his hands to the sides. 'Let her go, Coulter. You know it's all over, your men have been rounded up. Let her go, and I'll see you get out of this alive.'

Coulter gave a humourless laugh. 'You know that's a lie. But I shall get out alive, Turner, because you're going to help me. I don't need to tell you what happens if you don't.'

'What do you want?'

'You put me on the eastbound train, and disable the telegraph. Simple.' He reached out one foot and touched a carpet bag alongside Betsy. 'It will be hard to leave the Blue Diamond behind, but there's enough in there to see me started again.'

Matt began to back towards the door. 'All right, I'll go and talk to Marshal Brand—'

'No. You'll talk to no one. This is just between you and me. We'll go out by the back and walk down to the depot. Betsy here will walk at my side the whole way. And she'll get on the train with me. Just to ensure that you and your friends don't try anything.'

Sally's wailing had faded to a moan. Coulter glanced at her. 'We won't need you any more Sally, you can go now.'

The woman seemed not to hear, but just went on rocking, the blood dripping silently from her hands to form a little puddle on the floor. Sickened, Matt returned his attention to Coulter.

'Listen Duke,' he said urgently, 'take the knife away from Betsy's throat. I'll do whatever you want, I swear it.' He gestured at the weapons that lay on the bed. 'You've got my gun, use that. You can't hold that knife steady while we walk down the street. If you so much as stumble you're a dead man, because I'll kill you if you hurt her, and I don't need a gun or a knife to do it. You know that.'

Coulter seemed to consider what Matt had said, and finally he nodded his head. 'All right. Take a couple of steps back.' Matt obeyed, retreating to the doorway. Coulter picked up Monty's pistol with his left hand, holding it out above Betsy's head so it was pointing at Matt. With a move so fast it was almost undetectable he slid the stiletto up his sleeve, and began to bring his right hand across to join the other.

It was what Matt had been waiting for. His gun hand flashed round behind his back and came back holding Ches Marryat's revolver, cocked and ready to fire. The crack of the shot was thunderously loud in the small room. A small black hole appeared in the middle of Duke Coulter's forehead, and he toppled slowly sideways. Like Matt Turner, Coulter was right handed, and the pistol dropped harmlessly from his left.

A moment later Betsy was in Matt's arms, hugging him tight, her body trembling. 'You could have got yourself killed,' she scolded.

'What, me? No chance,' he replied, resting his face against her hair and drinking in the scent of her. 'But you sure had me worried. You're not hurt?'

'No, I'm fine. Just fine.' Betsy thrust him quickly away and dropped to her knees beside Sally, her arm draped protectively over the woman's bare shoulders, her hair with its first sprinkle of grey mingling with the brassy fake blonde. Matt grinned, his eyes moist. Yes, Betsy was fine. About the finest woman a man could wish for.